DOLPHIN SONG

'transports you instantly into the heart of Africa and the landscape so beautifully evoked in her first children's book, *The White Giraffe* . . . beguiling storytelling with a timeless feel.'
The Bookseller

'vivid and lyrical'
Publishing News

'stirring stuff'
Daily Telegraph

'another stunning novel'
Angels and Urchins

DOLPHIN SONG

LAUREN St JOHN

Illustrated by David Dean

Orion
Children's Books

First published in Great Britain in 2007
by Orion Children's Books
a division of the Orion Publishing Group Ltd
Orion House
5 Upper St Martin's Lane
London WC2H 9EA
An Hachette Livre UK Company

3 5 7 9 10 8 6 4

A catalogue record for this book is available
from the British Library

Printed in Great Britain by Clays Ltd, St Ives plc

ISBN 978 1 84255 533 0

www.orionbooks.co.uk

For my godson, Francis,
who is not quite old enough to read this book
but who loves dolphins and sharks with "big teef".

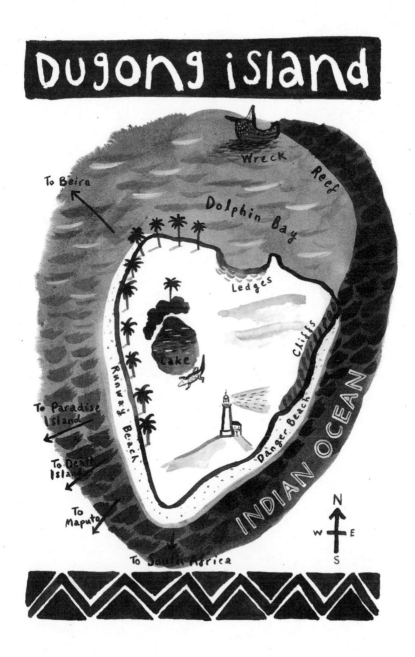

· 1 ·

When her teacher first told the class that they were going on an ocean voyage to see the 'Sardine Run', Martine Allen had a funny vision of the silver, tomato sauce-covered sardines that come in cans, only whole and wearing matching silver trainers in which they'd sprint along the South African coast.

But that wasn't it at all. The Sardine Run was, Miss Volkner told them, one of the greatest wildlife spectacles on earth. It was a migration by sea. Every June and July, millions of sardines left their home off the Aghulas banks on the west coast of South Africa in pursuit of their main food, the nutrient-rich plankton flowing

1

eastwards on the cold current. The sardines swam after the plankton with their mouths open, gobbling it up as they went. They in turn were pursued by tens of thousands of predators, including dolphins, dusky, ragged tooth, and bronze whaler sharks, and great flocks of Cape gannets with fledgling chicks.

Joining this caravan would be Martine and her classmates. Miss Volkner explained that they would follow the Sardine Run up the KwaZulu-Natal coast, before continuing north to Mozambique, where they would help count the population of dugongs.

'What are dugongs?' Martine whispered to Sherilyn Meyer, and was told that they were those 'cute, lumpy, grey things . . . You know, sort of like a cross between a hippo and a seal. The old sailors used to think they were mermaids.'

The whole class was in a fever of excitement at the thought of ten whole days off school in mid-term, and on a cruise ship no less. So was Martine, until her teacher handed round some notes on the trip. Top of the list of what to pack was:

1 Swimming Costume

Martine put up her hand. 'Excuse me, Miss Volkner, but why do we need a swimming costume?'

There was a lot of giggling, and Miss Volkner couldn't resist a smile. 'It's called a *sea* voyage because we're going to sea, Martine,' she said. 'There'll be endless opportunities to snorkel, dive and splash around in the waves, and I don't think we want you swimming without a costume!'

More laughter.

'But what if . . . ' Martine tried to get the wording right, ' . . . what if some of us preferred not to swim?'

'Why ever would you not want to get into the water?' asked a surprised Miss Volkner. 'The reefs are glorious. Trust me, Martine, once you've swum in the open ocean, where the seabed might be as much as half a mile beneath you, we won't be able to keep you out of the water.'

Somebody else asked a question then, so nobody noticed that the colour had drained from Martine's face and that, beneath her desk, her knees had started to tremble.

That night, the sharks came for Martine for the first time. They circled her in technicolour nightmares, their deep-set dead eyes on her flapping white limbs as she struck out across tempestuous seas. Over the weeks, the dreams increased in frequency and intensity to such an extent that Martine became afraid to go to sleep. Two nights before she was due to leave on the school trip, she took the extreme measure of sitting up in bed with a stack of books on her head so that they'd crash to the floor and wake her if she nodded off. Unfortunately, by then she was so exhausted that the third time they toppled she barely heard them. She simply scooted down in the sheets and gave herself up to the sharks.

She was battling to stay afloat and uneaten in an ocean so icy that her limbs felt paralyzed, when a disembodied voice cut into her dream. 'Wakey wakey, Martine! We'll need to go soon if we want to get to the beach while it's still early.'

Martine forced herself into consciousness. It was morning and a blurry figure was sitting on the edge of her bed. She blinked and it swam into focus. Her grandmother, dressed, as usual, in denim jeans but wearing a pale blue shirt instead of her khaki work one with the lion on the pocket, was watching her with sharp indigo eyes.

'How many times have I told you not to sleep with the window open?' Gwyn Thomas reproached her gently. 'No wonder you have nightmares. You're freezing. June is winter in Africa, Martine. Try to remember that.'

Martine struggled to free herself from the cold tentacles of her dream. 'I was drowning,' she said blearily. 'There were sharks and I couldn't breathe.'

'*Of course* you were drowning,' said Gwyn Thomas, leaning forward and briskly shutting out the biting, antelope-tinged air. 'You were all caught up in the blankets. And what are these books doing on the floor?'

Martine disentangled herself and sat up. She didn't want to worry her grandmother by telling her how bad the nightmares had become. 'I was trying to find something good to read.'

'And you thought you'd start with *The Enthusiast's*

Guide to Model Railways and the *Jeep Engine Repair Handbook*?'

Martine didn't answer. She was too absorbed by the view from her bedroom window. Beneath the thatched eaves, a herd of elephants straggled around the distant waterhole, grey ghosts in the wintry dawn mist. She'd been at Sawubona for six months now, and she still couldn't believe she lived on a game reserve in South Africa; still got a thrill every single morning when she opened her eyes, propped herself up on one elbow and looked out over the savannah wilderness she now called home. Those things didn't take away the knot of sadness that had dwelled inside her ever since her mum and dad had died in a New Year's Eve blaze in their Hampshire home in England, but they definitely helped.

It helped, too, that she had a new family. It wasn't a replacement family, because no one could ever replace the parents she'd worshipped. But at least she didn't feel so isolated anymore. Along with her grandmother, there was Tendai, the big Zulu who had recently been promoted from tracker to game warden. Tendai taught her bushcraft skills to help her survive the beautiful but deadly African landscape, and took her for campfire breakfasts up on the game reserve escarpment. Martine adored Tendai, but she had a very special relationship with his aunt, Grace, an African medicine woman and traditional healer – a *sangoma* – who also happened to be the best cook in the world. Grace's ancestors were both African and Caribbean and she alone knew the secret of Martine's gift with animals, and many other secrets besides.

Last, and to Martine's mind, most important, was her white giraffe, Jeremiah (Jemmy for short). Martine thought of Jemmy, who she'd tamed and could ride, and Ben, the boy who'd helped her rescue the white giraffe when he was stolen, as her best friends, although since Jemmy couldn't talk and Ben was mostly silent, they hadn't actually confirmed that.

'Some time today would be nice,' Gwyn Thomas said pointedly, and Martine remembered that she was supposed to be getting up. She glanced at the bedside clock and stifled a groan. Six a.m.! Sometimes she wished her grandmother was more of a fan of Sunday morning lie-ins.

Gwyn Thomas saw Martine's expression and her eyes sparkled with amusement. Once, those eyes had only ever studied Martine with coolness or hostility but these days her tanned face was more usually creased in a smile.

'You must be so excited about leaving on the school trip tomorrow,' she said. 'Ten whole days at sea. Ten whole days of history and nature and, I suppose, a little adventure. I envy you, I really do. I almost wish I was going with you.'

'Want to swap places?'

Gwyn Thomas laughed. 'For a minute there, you sounded almost serious, Martine. You are looking forward to it, aren't you?'

'Absolutely,' said Martine with as much conviction as she could muster. She swallowed a yawn. 'Can't wait.'

'I'm glad to hear it, because you've been looking quite pale recently. You could do with some sea air. Well, I'll see you downstairs in a few minutes. I'm just packing a picnic for our beach walk.'

'See you downstairs,' Martine said brightly, but as soon as the door swung shut behind her grandmother, she put her head in her hands and closed her eyes. She knew very well why she was having the shark dreams and it had nothing to do with sleeping with her window open in winter, getting tangled up in blankets, eating cheese before bedtime, or any of the other things people said caused nightmares. She was getting them because of something that had happened almost exactly a year ago.

She and her parents had been on holiday in Cornwall, England. On their last afternoon there Martine's dad, a doctor, had received an emergency call to help some boys who'd fallen down a cliff. Martine's mum, Veronica, was recovering from a bout of flu and was having an afternoon nap, and her dad had asked Martine if she would mind reading or drawing for a while because he wanted her mum to get plenty of rest.

But it was a roasting hot day and after a while Martine was bored and decided that if she nipped down to the beach and put her toes in the sea, she could be back before her mum woke up. When she got down there, though, the water was so inviting that soon she was up to her knees and then her waist. Then, out of nowhere, a wave had knocked her flat. It had dragged her along the seabed and she'd tumbled over and over as if she was in the spin cycle of a washing machine. When she felt certain she would drown, the wave had ejected her forcibly, and she'd managed to half swim, half crawl back to the beach.

At more or less the same time, a fisherman had pulled in a basking shark. Martine had seen its sinister shape on the sand as she staggered up the beach and somehow the two things had become combined in her mind – the shark and the washing-machine wave. Moments later she was in her mum's arms. Veronica, who'd been searching high and low for her, was so ecstatic to see her safe that she forgot to scold her. Not wanting to distress her mum further, Martine had thought it best not to mention the wave and how she'd nearly drowned, although she did vow to herself that she would never again swim in the sea if she could help it.

None of that had mattered until now because they'd left Cornwall the next day, and her parents had died before they could have another seaside holiday. As a result, nobody had found out about the one thing Martine had never confessed to another living soul because she didn't even want to admit it to herself. She was petrified of deep water.

2

In the six months she'd been in South Africa Martine had not once been to the beach because her grandmother rarely left the Storm Crossing area and wasn't the sort of person who would ever be caught covered in sunblock, reclining on a striped deckchair. For obvious reasons, Martine was quite content with this arrangement, so she'd been taken aback the previous evening when Gwyn Thomas had suggested that they get up at dawn and go for a walk along the Cape coast. Luckily it was far too cold to swim, so swimming wasn't an issue, which meant that Martine was much more enthusiastic about the idea than she would have been had it been summer.

She was even more pleased when they reached Uiserfontein shortly before eight that Sunday morning and she saw the ocean spilling out before her. The sun was a band of glittering gold splayed across a heaving wilderness of metallic blue. Purple heather grew right up to the shore. As she climbed out of the car, the sea breeze snatched at her scarf and the smell of the waves filled her nostrils.

It was definitely not warm and Martine was glad her grandmother had insisted she 'rug up' with a woolly hat, windcheater and gloves. Seagulls aside, there was no one around but a kite surfer out in the bay. Martine stood riveted on the dunes as he rode the waves like a charioteer. At intervals he'd disappear behind a swell and all that would be visible was his kite, a billowing parachute in candy-coloured stripes. He'd be gone for so long that she'd begin to think he'd fallen victim to the undertow, but then he'd come speeding out on the face of a breaker.

The wind whipped the waves into powdery plumes of spray, like the manes of white horses. They'd toss the man and his board into the air, and the kite would catch him and lift him even higher, allowing him to somersault and twist in effortless defiance of gravity. Then he'd float back down and slip behind another swell.

Out on the beach, the whistling wind made conversation difficult and Martine couldn't help thinking about the school trip again. Her swimming fears aside, it did sound fantastic. Miss Volkner had told the class that the Sardine Run was one of the great wonders of the natural world, as marvellous a migration as that of the wildebeest in East Africa, where every year over a million of the curly-horned beasts moved in an epic black sweep across the yellow plains of the Serengeti, evading lions, hyenas, the spotted gold streaks which were hunting cheetahs, and slow-blinking crocodiles in torrential rivers. On the Sardine Run, she said, it was not uncommon for shoals of sardines to be as much as fifteen kilometres long and three kilometres wide, and for the pods of dolphins which pursued them to be a thousand-strong.

Martine was looking forward to the dolphins most of all. She had only ever seen one dolphin in real life and that was at a grim aquarium she'd visited with her equally grim former school, Bodley Brook. In a peeling swimming pool, a trainer had coaxed it into performing dozens of tricks with beach balls and rubber rings. Some of the children had been invited to reward it with fish from a bucket – probably sardines – but Martine had kept her distance. When the dolphin approached the poolside she'd noticed that its mouth was curled at the corners in a permanent smile. Throughout the show, she'd had the feeling that the dolphin was smiling only because it couldn't help it – like a clown smiling through tears.

The dolphin memory reminded her of another animal she felt was being taken advantage of: her own white giraffe. The best thing about Jemmy becoming famous after the rescue was that he'd lost his currency to hunters. As the only white giraffe on earth, he was still very valuable, but not nearly as valuable as he had been when he was a mythical beast of legend. And he was not exactly of a size which would make it easy for a poacher to catch him and dye him a different colour for reasons of disguise.

The *worst* thing about Jemmy becoming famous was that everyone wanted to see him. Previously, he'd slept in his secret sanctuary during the day and only come out at night. Now, he went there at night and roamed the game reserve during the day, and Gwyn Thomas led White Giraffe tours around Sawubona in search of him. She had even ordered White Giraffe mugs and White Giraffe T-shirts.

Over the past few months, Martine and her grandmother's relationship had improved about a thousand per cent, but the White Giraffe tours were a bone of contention. Gwyn Thomas organized them very carefully so that Jemmy would not be stressed in the least, but Martine loathed the idea of camera-laden tourists gawking at Jemmy. She had made her feelings on the subject very clear. She'd begged and pleaded for the tours to stop and gone on and on about how sensitive and special Jemmy was, but her grandmother was adamant that the best way to ensure that the white giraffe stayed special was to allow people access to him in a controlled environment. Added to which, the game reserve needed the money he earned them.

'It's simple arithmetic, Martine. The more money we can make, the more animals we can save.'

And there was nothing Martine could say to that

because times were tough at Sawubona and she, too, wanted to save as many animals as possible.

A mitten-covered hand tugged at her sleeve. She realized that her grandmother was trying to get her attention.

'Honestly, Martine, I sometimes think your hearing's worse than mine. I haven't got my glasses with me. What's that on the beach up ahead? Is it a seal? Or is it just an oddly-shaped rock?'

Martine blocked out the sun's bright rays with her hand. She gasped. 'I think . . . I think it's a dolphin.'

Martine reached the dolphin first. Gwyn Thomas later commented that she would never have believed her granddaughter – hopeless at all sports bar giraffe-riding – was capable of moving at such a speed, had she not witnessed it herself. But Martine slowed for the last few steps so as not to alarm the dolphin if it was still alive.

It was, but if appearances were anything to go by, not for much longer.

Martine crouched by the edge of the water and two things happened at once. She looked into the dolphin's dark blue irises and had the curious sensation she was falling into them – into a place of wisdom beyond understanding and innocence beyond measure; and not only that, but that it wanted to communicate with her. Simultaneously, she put her hands on its shining grey body, expecting it to have a cold, rubbery feel, and found instead that it was satin-smooth and muscular. When she stroked it a bolt of electricity ran up her arms, just as it had when she'd first touched the white giraffe. She snatched her palms away as if she'd been scorched.

'The poor thing has beached itself,' said her grandmother, hurrying up. 'It's a real mystery why they do that, but it's happening more and more. Only the other week I was reading about 300 dolphins stranded on the shore in Zanzibar. Martine? Martine, are you all right? You're as white as snow. If this is too upsetting for you, you can wait in the car while I get help.'

Martine found her voice. 'What do we do? How do we save it? How will it breathe?'

'Well, dolphins are mammals not fish so they breathe oxygen like us, but shock and being out of the water are what kills them. We need to keep its skin wet. There's a bucket in the car. You're a lot younger and fitter than I am. Would you run and get it, and fetch my mobile, too. I'll call the marine rescue department. Isn't it amazing how that wretched phone is never handy when you need it?'

Martine stood up reluctantly. The dolphin was dying and it had as good as asked for her help. If she did as her grandmother requested it would take time – time that might mean the difference between life and death. If she attempted to save the dolphin herself she could start immediately, but there were two big hurdles. The first was that she'd never tried healing a dolphin before. What if she couldn't do it and she had wasted a crucial half hour which could have been used to summon the marine rescue people and the dolphin died and it was her fault? The second was that her grandmother didn't know about her gift. She did know about the Zulu legend which said that the child who could ride a white giraffe would have power over all the animals, but she had never seen any evidence of it and she didn't really know what it meant.

'It's a shame that any powers you've been given don't extend to keeping your room tidy, Martine,' she liked to joke.

Not even Martine knew what the legend meant. All she knew was that she had to find an excuse to get her grandmother out of the way.

'Martine, this *is* an emergency!' Gwyn Thomas reminded her.

A family of dog walkers spilled into view. They were moving down the creamy beach in the opposite direction, pulled by a trio of exuberant black Labradors.

'Those people might have a phone,' Martine suggested. 'It might be quicker if we ask them to call the marine rescue services.'

'Good thinking, dear. Why don't you run and ask them.'

'I can't,' Martine said. She hung her head in what she hoped was a bashful way. 'I'm shy. Please can I stay here with the dolphin?'

A germ of a suspicion crossed Gwyn Thomas's face. 'You're shy?'

'Yes.'

'I would have thought that this was one time when . . . Oh, never mind. Well, try to keep it calm while I'm gone.'

Martine waited until her grandmother was well on her way to the dog walkers before laying her hands on the dolphin's silky-smooth body again. Its skin was dry and warm. Once again, the electric current zapped her but this time she was ready for it. She kept her palms on the dolphin's side, and in her head she apologized to it for not knowing anything about the healing of dolphins. Nothing happened at first, but then her palms heated up to the point where they were almost sizzling, her heart felt full to bursting, and into her mind came a vision – not of tribesmen in animal masks and swirling smoke and great herds of buffalo and giraffe, as she'd experienced when she'd tried healing before, but of an island with white sand. And in the aquamarine waters which surrounded it, she saw herself quite clearly, swimming with dolphins.

'Is it dead?'

Martine jerked back to reality to find that her jeans were soaked through, as if she'd been waist-deep in water. The kite surfer was standing over her. 'Excuse me?' she murmured vaguely.

'Is it dead?' he repeated a little impatiently.

Martine shook her head, as much to snap herself out of her trance as in reply. She heard herself say, 'No, it was just resting. Would you mind helping me put it back into the sea?'

The kite surfer was powerfully built and he used the lines from his kite to assist him, but it took every ounce of their combined strength to pull, push and roll the dolphin into the ocean. Submerged in water, the dolphin made no attempt to swim. It sank slowly.

Martine's heart sank with it.

'I thought you said it was just resting?' the kite surfer said a little accusingly.

The dolphin gave an experimental twitch of its tail, then a more vigorous wiggle. It surfaced, tipped on its side and regarded Martine with inquisitive eyes. It flapped a fin, sent some cheerful squeaks and clicks in her direction, and was gone in a shining streak. When next she saw it, it was performing acrobatics in the far breakers.

The kite surfer chuckled. 'Funny thing about dolphins,' he said, 'ever noticed that you can't help smiling when you're around them?'

He picked up his board and departed with a friendly salute. Martine waded out of the icy water and wrung out the bottoms of her wet jeans, her hands tingling. She felt elated. Her gift had allowed her to help a wild dolphin. What else would it allow her to do? It seemed to be a gift of healing and communication. She didn't feel as if it belonged to her, though. She felt as if she was the caretaker of it. A sort of conductor.

Watching the dolphin dive gleefully over a wave, Martine found that the kite surfer was right. She couldn't keep from smiling. However, when her grandmother homed into sight, she hastily rearranged her expression.

'Well, that was a waste of time,' Gwyn Thomas reported as she strode up, bucket swinging. 'They had no phone so I did have to go to the car after all. Really, Martine, I think it might have been kind if you'd volunteered to do it for me. I'm not as fit as I used to be. Good heavens, you're soaking! What were you thinking of, going in the Atlantic in mid-winter? You'll end up with pneumonia.'

She did a double take. '*Where* is the dolphin?'

Martine pointed out into the bay. 'There,' she said, unable to suppress a grin.

'But how?' asked her grandmother, bewildered. 'I don't understand.'

Martine shrugged. 'The kite surfer came by and he helped me put the dolphin back into the sea. Then it just swam away.'

'Just like that, huh? It just swam away?'

'That's right.'

'Hmmm.'

Gwyn Thomas stared at her with a mixture of puzzled admiration and something else which Martine couldn't quite fathom, but which gave her a warm feeling inside. It was obvious that her grandmother wanted to probe further, but for some reason she resisted the urge. 'Come on, you,' was all she said, 'let's get you out of those wet things.'

They were almost at the car when Martine realized that, if she was soaked to the waist, she must have waded or swum in the sea during her trance. The odd thing was that she hadn't been afraid. She hadn't been afraid at all.

3

To Martine, almost the best part about the whole dolphin rescue was the drive home. Her grandmother knew that something had happened; she just wasn't quite sure what. The invisible barrier between them, which had to do with the pain of past memories – mainly those concerning Martine's mum – dropped away, and the bond they did have, which was about a shared love of animals, deepened. Every so often Gwyn Thomas would mimic Martine saying, 'And then it just swam away!' and they'd both laugh.

That feeling of closeness lasted until precisely 5:47 p.m. when Martine came down from her room wearing jeans and boots and announced she was going out riding on the white giraffe.

'Not now, Martine,' her grandmother remarked casually, glancing up from her newspaper. 'I think you've had enough excitement for one day.'

'But I can't possibly go on the Sardine Run without saying goodbye to Jemmy,' said Martine, unable to comprehend that her grandmother might be serious. 'I *have* to see him, I just have to.'

'Then you should have done it earlier.' Gwyn Thomas lifted her newspaper as if to continue reading.

'But I didn't realize how late it was,' Martine said beseechingly.

Her grandmother was unsympathetic. 'Martine, it's already nearly dark and you know how I feel about you riding after sundown.'

Martine's blood began to boil. The ban on night riding was another big bone of contention between them. As far as Gwyn Thomas was concerned, the game reserve was simply too full of hunting predators after dark for riding the white giraffe at that time to be an option. She wasn't interested in Martine's explanation about how she was perfectly safe when she was on Jemmy's back because the other animals thought she was an extension of him.

'Besides,' continued her grandmother, 'you haven't even packed. No, don't look at me like that. I know you're disappointed but I promise I'll say goodbye to Jemmy for you. That's my final word on the matter. You're over-tired and if you don't get a decent night's sleep, you won't be in a fit state to enjoy the fantastic voyage Miss Volkner has planned for you. And that would be a real shame.'

Martine knew from bitter experience that when her grandmother used that particular tone of voice, argument was futile. But the idea of going away for ten whole days without riding Jemmy, or even saying goodbye to him, was too hideous to contemplate. She stewed about it all through dinner, pushing her roast chicken around the plate. Gwyn Thomas finally told her off for sulking. After that, Martine made an effort to sit up straight and be outwardly charming. Inside, she was hatching a plan. It had been months since she'd sneaked out after midnight to ride Jemmy, and she missed the exhilaration of those moonlit rides. Most of all, she missed the connection with Africa. Alone with the giraffe and the other wildlife, she'd felt as if she had opened a door on a hidden Africa, the Africa only a handful of people ever got to see.

Sitting at the table ladling gravy onto her crispy potatoes, Martine savoured the thrill of disobedience. She had always avoided being caught before, even when she was totally unfamiliar with the workings of Sawubona and her grandmother's routine. Now she was an expert on both. Now it should be simplicity itself.

Martine was almost giddy with anticipation. To divert her grandmother's attention, she turned the conversation back to the dolphin, asking her once more why a dolphin would drag itself ashore to almost certain death.

Relieved to have the tension broken, Gwyn Thomas

was more than willing to discuss the issue of dolphin beachings again, saying that she wasn't sure why they did it and could only imagine it was because something in the sea had made their life unbearable. 'It could be pollution or increased traffic in the oceans,' she said. 'Some parts of the sea have become virtual cities of ships, fishing trawlers and navy vessels, you know.'

Martine listened and tried to remember all the stories she'd heard over the years about the intelligence of dolphins, and how their mere presence could sometimes heal people from illness and trauma. She recalled the electric current that had passed through her when she touched the beached dolphin. Somehow, without words, it had appealed to her to help it. And somehow, without words, she'd agreed.

As a rule, Martine told her grandmother things on a need-to-know basis, and she had never confided in her about the silent dog-whistle she used to call the white giraffe. Consequently, she could now sit at her bedroom window blowing the whistle, without fear of detection, until Jemmy appeared at the skeleton tree near the waterhole.

When her grandmother's bedroom light went out, Martine took off her pyjamas and put on her jeans, boots, sweatshirt and windcheater. She removed her knife and torch from the survival kit she kept tucked behind the bookshelf and slipped downstairs. Jemmy was waiting for her at the game park gate, his white coat ghostly in the darkness. He lay down on the ground so she could climb onto his sloping, velvety back. 'Go, Jemmy,' she urged when she was on safely, and then he was up and galloping.

The winter wind blasted Martine's face but for once it didn't bother her. The rush of the illicit ride was too intoxicating. Riding in the daylight had its advantages – she was in a lot less danger and didn't have to sneak around for a start. But it did mean she had to ride more sedately. Her grandmother would have had a stroke if she saw how fast Jemmy went if he was allowed to. More importantly, it meant staying away from the Secret Valley, the sanctuary where the white giraffe had been taken as an orphan by the elephant who'd saved him from poachers.

It was the Secret Valley Martine was headed for tonight. For reasons she couldn't explain, she knew she had to see the cave which held the keys to her destiny before she left Sawubona. Unfortunately, it was not the easiest place to get to. The entrance was a crevice guarded by a twisted tree, draped with thorny creepers. The only way of negotiating the crevice was for Jemmy to gallop towards the tree at full speed and leap at exactly the right angle. She always found it difficult to stay on his back during the jump, and this time was no different. Vines and branches pricked, dragged and raked at her, and Martine could do little but bury her face in Jemmy's mane and cling on. She hoped the scratches weren't so bad that she'd be unable to explain them away in the morning.

Inside the valley, the fragrance of orchids still hung in the air, although they were no longer in bloom. A patch of star-scattered sky lent a bluey sheen to the dark of the grassy space. Martine slid off Jemmy's back and gave him a kiss of thanks. This was only the third time she'd been to the valley and she felt as jittery as ever about entering the creepy tunnel. Jemmy watched her go, ears flickering.

The narrow passage smelled musty and feral, as if a leopard had recently vacated it. Martine's torch cast a slender, wavering beam along its rough-hewn walls. After a few minutes, the tunnel widened and turned back on itself and she knew she was underneath the mountain once more. Clambering up the steep, mossy steps that led to the cave's antechamber, Martine felt annoyed with herself for not coming up with a plan to keep her jeans clean by, say, wrapping dustbin bags around them. She only had two pairs and both would be coming on the school trip in the morning.

Shortly before she reached the top, Martine turned off her torch. On her first visit, the bat colony which dangled with folded wings from the antechamber roof had gone berserk and got caught up in her hair. This time, fortunately, they didn't stir.

The 'Memory Room', as the ancients had called it, was before her. Martine switched on her torch as she entered the cave, and breathed in its weighty air. She loved the thickness of it. It was as if its very molecules were imprinted with the genetic codes of generations past. All around her were cave paintings capturing the lives and memories of a lost tribe of Bushmen, or San people as they were also known. Red, black and ochre sketches of great herds of wild animals, and men with bows and arrows, so vibrant that they could have been painted yesterday, seemed to spring to life as her torch danced over them. They galloped across the walls. Martine felt privileged to witness them. Coming to the cave, she always felt as though she was visiting her own personal art gallery.

She walked over to the paintings of the white giraffe. It was months since she'd last seen them, but she felt as if she carried them with her always. As if they were engraved on her heart. There were three pictures, but only one showed a child riding a white giraffe. The Bushmen artist had managed to capture Jemmy's exquisite coat exactly. It even shimmered the way Jemmy's did in real life.

So often had she revisited the cave in her head that at first she didn't register that there was something different about the line-up of images. She just stared at the wall in a daze. It was only gradually that she took in what she was looking at. Two new paintings had been added to the sequence!

Martine tried to work out whether it was possible for her to have missed them on a previous visit. She decided that it wasn't. They were slightly obscured by a pyramid-shaped rock, but she'd had the opportunity to study the other paintings twice, at length and at close range. On the second occasion Grace had been with her and *she* hadn't spotted them either. Or had she?

'The answers are right here on these walls,' the *sangoma* had told her, 'but only time and experience will give you eyes to see them.'

Martine touched the rock and felt its strange energy. It was wet. Her torch illuminated a trickle of water running down from a fissure. It provided an explanation of sorts; just not a very satisfactory one. Perhaps the paintings had been covered by a fine dust and a leak of rainwater had rinsed it away and revealed the image beneath. That was one possibility, anyway. Martine didn't buy it. She thought it more likely that Grace was right – only time and experience would allow her to see what she was meant to see.

In the first painting, twenty-one dolphins were lying side by side on a beach. Blood trickled from one dolphin's ear. The second painting was more of a pattern than a picture. It showed rings and rings of dolphins – more than a hundred of them by the look of it – surrounded by a large circle of sharks. There was something in the middle. Martine held up her torch and leaned closer. It was a swimmer. A swimmer surrounded by sharks and dolphins.

Martine's heart did an uncomfortable flip. She was caught in the middle of some ancient prophecy. The destiny that the forefathers had predicted or mapped out for her – she was never quite sure which – was in motion once more, carrying her with it like a leaf on a current. Martine wondered if it was possible to outrun fate. Her parents had tried it with catastrophic consequences, but maybe she could simply sidestep it. She would still go on the school trip but she would refuse to swim or go anywhere near the water, no matter what. Sharks were hardly going to climb up the side of the ship to get at her.

As if the forefathers were reaching out from beyond the grave, her torch fizzed and flicked. Martine, who had been trying to be brave from the moment she entered the claustrophobic tunnel, lost her nerve. She turned and fled. In her rush, she forgot about the bats and clattered down the rocky steps, torch beam swooping madly, startling them from their upside-down dreaming. Their silhouettes skittered across the rock walls like vampire wallpaper. Incensed squeaks, raised to the level of a cacophony by the echo, pursued her down the tunnel.

Back in the Secret Valley, Jemmy sensed her anxiety. He bolted almost before Martine was on his back, nearly unseating her as he crashed through the twisted tree. Clinging to his mane, Martine understood for the first time that she was never really in control of the white giraffe when she rode him; that she relied totally on the bond between them, on trust, on Jemmy's goodwill. If anything ever happened to change that, disaster would quickly follow. But, she told herself firmly, it wouldn't. So she leaned forward and let adrenalin course through her body and watched the dark shapes of a herd of browsing buffalo flash by.

When the white giraffe finally bounced to a halt in the trees near the waterhole, Martine slid to the ground and hugged him. His neck was wet with sweat. He put his head down and made his musical fluttering sound. Martine did her best to explain to him that she was going away for a little while, but that she'd be thinking of him constantly and loved him with all her heart.

Locking the game reserve gate behind her, Martine sprinted through the mango trees and perfumed gardenias. When she opened the back door, the silence of the house seemed to swirl out and envelope her. Perhaps because her nerves were still jangling from the wild ride, a sense of foreboding filled her. She stepped into the kitchen. The faint scent of roast chicken lingered. Moonlight fell in white streaks across the tiled floor. Martine stole past her grandmother's door and up the wooden staircase. Every creak sent her racing pulse into the stratosphere. When she reached her room, she didn't turn on the light but just sank onto the bed and exhaled.

She was unlacing her boots when she began to get the feeling that she wasn't alone. A stifled cough cut through the stillness. Martine leapt to her feet in fright.

A spectral figure was sitting in the wicker chair.

4

A switch clicked and Gwyn Thomas's face came at her abruptly out of the darkness. The lamplight lent it a yellow cast, shadowing her brow and throwing the lines around her mouth and eyes into harsh relief. She looked like an eagle owl. Martine stood there feeling her intestines writhe like snakes and her stomach shrink into a hard, sick ball. She could almost hear the fragile bond between her and her grandmother shatter.

'Have you had a good time?' her grandmother asked lightly. 'Have you enjoyed yourself galloping merrily around in the moonlight, unconcerned that I might be lying awake not knowing which might maul, maim or gore you first – a lion, leopard, rhino or bull elephant? Afraid that the phone might ring and it would be the night guard to tell me that you'd fallen off and broken every bone in your body, or been bitten by a Cape cobra, or savaged by a male baboon, or ripped to shreds by a hyena protecting its young.'

As if to support her case, a lion roared in the starlight. 'Shall I go on?'

'I'm sorry,' Martine said inadequately. Somehow the knowledge that none of this was an exaggeration – that, any time she went out into the game reserve with Jemmy, particularly at night, she was taking the risk that one or more of those things could happen to her – made the words harder to bear.

Her grandmother's face was a mask of fury and disappointment. 'Well, I'm sorry, Martine, but sorry is no longer good enough. My first inclination when I found that you had disobeyed me was to pull you off the school trip . . . '

Martine held her breath. It would be ironic if her grandmother's punishment played into her hands by taking her off the school trip.

' . . . But that,' her grandmother continued, 'would be a slap in the face of Miss Volkner and everyone else who has worked so hard to put the voyage together. And I think it will do you the power of good to be away from Sawubona and the white giraffe for a while. You seem to have lost all sight of the fact that, although you have a special relationship with Jemmy, he is a wild animal and wild animals are unpredictable. To help remind you of that detail, I'm going to ban you from riding him or even entering the reserve for six weeks after you return.'

'No!' cried Martine. '*Anything* but that. I'll get up at five every morning and do the household chores; I'll wash all the dishes or do all the ironing; I'll even clean the sanctuary animals' cages for a month. But please don't take me away from Jemmy. He needs me and I can't live without him. I'll die.'

Gwyn Thomas started for the door. 'Don't be melodramatic, Martine. Jemmy will manage just fine without you and, at the rate you're going, you'll live a lot longer without him. The discussion is closed. A six week ban and that's final.'

In that instant, all the hurts long forgotten, all the times when her grandmother had seemed not to want her or snapped at her or sent her to her room, all her frustration over Jemmy being gawped at by tourists, came boiling to the surface of Martine's mind. Combined with this fresh injustice, they caused an explosion. 'I HATE YOU, GWYN THOMAS!' she screamed.

Her grandmother swung round as if to hurl a bitter retort, but caught herself just as swiftly. Her shoulders seemed suddenly to sag. 'We'll be leaving at eight sharp in the morning. Make sure you're ready,' was all she said. The lights-switch clicked and she was gone.

Darkness closed in on Martine. Somehow the noisiness of Africa's night creatures – the hunting lions, the crickets, frogs and night birds – which she found so thrilling usually, made the silence in the house more terrible. The cruel words lingered in the air. Martine was wracked with equal parts of shame and resentment. She tried, and failed, to picture two whole months without Jemmy: the school trip plus the six-week punishment. She was quite sure she'd be eaten up by loneliness – that the loneliness would devour her, millimetre by millimetre, like a flesh-eating bug, until there was nothing left.

It was almost morning before she fell into a restless sleep plagued with visions of circling sharks, and this time they were closer than ever.

Breakfast was a tense and tasteless affair of hard-boiled eggs and toast, after which she and her grandmother drove to the school in silence.

'I think you need to think long and hard about your behaviour while you're away,' Gwyn Thomas said as she lifted Martine's bag from the boot of the car. 'And when you come back, we'll have to discuss your future at Sawubona.'

They stood staring at each another for a long moment – Martine yearning so badly for her grandmother to take her in her arms and make her feel loved and okay and not like the worst person in the whole world that it was a physical ache in her chest. But Gwyn Thomas merely laid an impersonal hand on her shoulder.

'Goodbye, Martine,' she said. 'See you soon.' Then she climbed into her battered red Datsun and drove away.

It took all the self-control Martine possessed not to run after the car. Instead she walked pale and wretched into the rose-lined school courtyard, where the rest of her class were chatting and fooling around in the morning sunshine. Usually Martine loved the aroma wafting from the canteen, but today it made her feel nauseous. She began to wish that she hadn't forced down the boiled eggs.

'Cheer up, Martine, it might never happen,' called out Claudius Rapier, who was lounging at one of the rustic wooden tables, a can of Coke in his hand. His friends laughed raucously.

Martine gave him the most withering look she was capable of. She wanted to tell him that something *had* happened and that even if it hadn't, nothing put her in a bad mood faster than people telling her to cheer up. But she knew it wasn't worth it. In a war of words, Claudius always came out on top.

Claudius had been at Caracal Junior for little more than a term but already he was the self-appointed leader of the 'Five Star Gang', a group of the most popular kids in school. He'd replaced Xhosa Washington, who had transferred to a school in Johannesburg after his father, the local mayor, was jailed for his part in assisting Sawubona's last game warden to smuggle rare animals out of South Africa.

Like Xhosa, there was something princely about Claudius, but unlike the mayor's son, he wasn't muscle-bound. He was overweight – fat even – in a country full of athletes, but that didn't seem to bother him. He had the permanent serene smile of someone upon whom fortune had always smiled, and for whom money had always smoothed every path and made all things possible. He had long blond hair, curling up at the ends, and, in spite of the fact that he existed entirely on fast food (the family chauffeur brought a selection of it to him piping hot each lunchtime), clear gold skin with a slight flush to it. Life was one long joke to him.

'Hey, Martine,' he said again, nodding at her jeans, which were ripped at both knees. 'We know you're an orphan, but do you have to dress the part?'

Before she could answer there was a commotion at the table behind him. The enormous breakfast which he and his friends had been about to tuck into, a feast of bacon double cheeseburgers, jam donuts, chocolate-chip cookies, strawberry milkshakes and coffee lattés in Styrofoam cups, was now lying on the courtyard lawn, beneath the ketchup-covered newspaper they'd been using as a tablecloth.

'Who did this?' roared Claudius, as his friends leapt to their feet with cries of distress. Martine couldn't help giggling, but really she was as startled as he was. There was no wind and nobody near the Five's table. The closest person to it was Ben Khumalo, the enigmatic half Indian, half Zulu boy, but he was at least thirty yards away, studying a noticeboard pinned to the canteen door. He had his back to them and his body language was relaxed, as if he'd been there for quite some time. He took a pen from his pocket and wrote something on an A4 sheet on the board.

Claudius glared at him for several seconds before apparently concluding that Ben was too far away and too much of a wimp to have performed so audacious an act.

He reached for his mobile phone. '*Moenie*, panic *nie*, my friends,' he said grandly. 'Don't panic. We'll order some more.'

'Everyone on the bus,' boomed Miss Volkner. 'We're leaving in five minutes.'

'Well, thank you very much,' Claudius said loudly to no one in particular. 'Thank you, whoever you are, for ruining my morning.'

Martine couldn't be sure but she thought she saw Ben wink.

· 5 ·

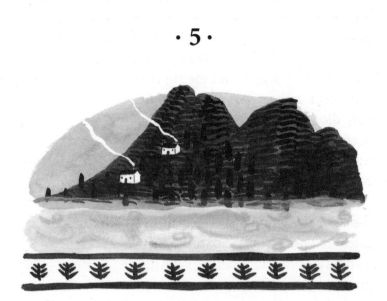

It was Ben who Martine chose to sit beside on the bus to Cape Town. She gave him a wan smile as she slid onto the seat, but didn't say anything. Ben never spoke at school, and she respected that. A lot of people thought Ben was mute – although some kids claimed to have once seen him having a perfectly normal conversation with his parents – and it made Martine feel good to share a secret with him, to know that whenever they were alone together, Ben talked to her quite freely, and that he spoke much more eloquently than anyone else she knew.

The teachers didn't mind that Ben didn't say anything because he had impeccable manners and always did his work well and on time, and Martine had never asked him why he didn't communicate with their classmates because it made perfect sense to her. Their conversations were all hot air. They talked about fashion and pop music and TV shows and the superficial, and sometimes just plain embarrassing, lives of the rich and famous. Ben didn't waste energy on words. He was a nature person like Tendai, happiest when he was outdoors. He was, thought Martine, a bit like a giraffe, mostly silent but no less extraordinary for it.

With a hiss of air brakes, the bus pulled slowly down the driveway and out of Caracal Junior's lynx-decorated gates. Tall pines slipped past the window. With no one to distract her, Martine sank quickly into a depression. Her grandmother's words went round and round in her head: 'When you return, Martine, we'll have to discuss your future at Sawubona.' What did that mean? Had she made up her mind overnight that she didn't want the responsibility of an eleven-year-old after all and decided she would just pack her off to a children's home in grey, rainy England? To boarding school? To foster parents?

And yet who could blame her?

Martine felt sick to her stomach when she remembered how she'd screamed like a demon child at her grandmother, 'I hate you, Gwyn Thomas!' She wished life came with a rewind button. If that was the case, she'd be feeling very differently now. She'd still be upset about not being allowed to see Jemmy, but maybe if she had apologized a bit more sincerely and promised faithfully never to sneak out at night again, her grandmother might have relented. She would have realized that keeping Martine and Jemmy apart for anything more than a week or two was like trying to separate Siamese twins.

Then, thought Martine, she and Gwyn Thomas would have parted with hugs and smiles and the special feeling they'd had after the dolphin rescue. Her grandmother wouldn't have been left believing that Martine hated her, when really the opposite was true. Martine loved her. She had just never found the right time to say it.

Her reverie was interrupted by a commotion at the back of the bus. Most of the kids were out of their seats. They were pointing at something outside and shrieking noisily.

'What's going on?' demanded Miss Volkner. 'We've hardly left the school gates and already you're up to no good.' She pushed between them. 'What on earth . . . ?'

Martine twisted round and was startled to see – through the dust-speckled window – Grace rushing after the bus, signalling for it to stop. She seemed to be carrying something. For a woman of her extravagant proportions, she moved with astonishing speed and, well, grace. Her billowing scarlet, orange and black African traditional dress made her an arresting spectacle.

Relief flooded through Martine. Grace might have a message from her grandmother. She levered open a side window. 'Grace!' she yelled. 'Grace!'

Miss Volkner raised her eyebrows. 'Do you know this person?'

'That's Grace,' Martine answered with pride. 'She's my friend.'

'Strange company you keep, Martine,' remarked Lucy van Heerden with a smirk. She tossed her silky blonde hair over her shoulder, and cast a disdainful glance at Ben. 'But then you always did like really peculiar people.'

Martine paid no attention to her.

'Be quiet, Lucy,' snapped Miss Volkner. 'I'm not sure why this friend of yours is pursuing the bus, Martine, but I'm afraid we can't stop to find out. If you've forgotten something, it's too bad. You'll just have to manage without it.'

'Oh, you have to stop, Miss Volkner,' implored Martine. 'You just have to.'

'I don't *have* to do anything, Martine. Try to understand that it's out of my hands. If we're not there on time, the boat will leave without us. Is that what you want?'

'I'll be really quick. Grace wouldn't have come unless it was an emergency. And she definitely wouldn't be running. What if something's happened at Sawubona?'

Miss Volkner pursed her lips. 'In the half hour or so that has elapsed since you left Sawubona, I very much doubt all the animals have escaped . . . '

Her voice trailed off. 'Oh, for goodness' sake, never let it be said I'm not fair. You have one minute. I mean it, one minute and that's it.'

She called to the driver and the bus stopped so abruptly that Martine was almost catapulted through the windscreen. The doors popped open. Martine jumped onto the verge, dew soaking her socks and trainers. Grace was waiting for her, still out of breath from her run. Her volcano-bright headscarf was unravelling and her rich brown skin glowed. She looked like a magnificent bird which had been subjected to some undignified ritual. She was holding a small rubbery plant with orange flowers.

'What's wrong, Grace?' asked Martine, speaking rapidly in the hope of getting information in the shortest time possible. 'Is everything okay? Has something happened at Sawubona? Have you been speaking to my grandmother?'

But Grace, straightening her headscarf, and checking the health of the plant, took her time answering. Vital seconds passed. Martine glanced over her shoulder and Miss Volkner tapped her watch. 'Be-Ware,' Grace said at last.

'Beware?' echoed Martine. 'Beware of what?'

'Tha boat fence. Watch out for tha boat fence.'

'I don't understand,' said Martine. '*What* boat fence?'

'That's it!' Miss Volkner interrupted. 'Time's up. Onto the bus THIS VERY SECOND or I'm removing your bags and leaving you behind.'

Grace thrust the plant at Martine. 'This here is a present for you.'

Martine took it uncertainly. 'Umm, thanks, Grace. What do you mean by . . . ?'

'I take it that you'd prefer to stay here?' Miss Volkner demanded, her voice shrill with exasperation. 'Driver, open the luggage compartment and we'll remove Martine's bag.'

Grace gave Martine a squeeze and a shove. 'Go, chile.

When tha time comes, you will know what to do.'

The bus was already moving when Martine leapt on board. The doors snapped shut. Grace's fiery plumage vanished in a swirl of dust.

Carrying the little plant, Martine walked the gauntlet of eyes down the aisle of the bus. She was bemused by Grace's warning and more than a little annoyed with Miss Volkner for wrenching her away before she could hear what the *sangoma* had come to say. It was obviously very important. Now she would never know. Now she would have to sail up one of the most treacherous coastlines in the world, unsure of what Grace had been trying to protect her from.

'Any other stops you'd like to make, Martine?' Claudius called. 'Should we pop into the game ranch? Or perhaps you'd like to pay a visit to all the other relatives and acquaintances you haven't seen recently? Don't mind us. We'll just come along for the ride.'

Martine could feel a beetroot flush spreading up her neck. She speeded up to get past her tormentor and her foot caught the handle of a sports bag. She tripped and the plant shot into the air. Martine almost did the same, but she managed to grab a seat-back and right herself. Claudius snatched the plant off the floor. He held it between his thumb and forefinger and regarded it with a comical expression of distaste. 'I didn't know you were a vegetarian,' he said to Martine. 'Hey, Sherilyn, have a bite of this!'

Before she could stop him, he'd tossed it across the aisle, where its gritty roots caught in Sherilyn's hair. Sherilyn gave a screech and batted it away. Luke caught it and threw it on, and after that it did the rounds of the bus, to the accompaniment of hoots and laughter. Martine tried pleading for its return but finally gave up and went to her seat, hot tears pricking the backs of her eyes.

'I don't know what's going on back there, but I've had about as much as I can take for one morning!' warned Miss Volkner from her seat beside the driver. 'If I hear so much as a squeak between here and Cape Town, we're turning the bus around and going back to Caracal Junior and you'll all spend the rest of the month in detention.'

Martine sat down beside Ben, avoiding his gaze. The gruelling morning had been too much for her. A few tears escaped and splashed onto the leather seat. Embarrassed, she rubbed her eyes roughly. When she opened them again, Ben was holding out a faded red bandana. Martine took it from him gratefully. She held the soft cloth against her face and somehow the clean cotton smell of it and Ben's simple act of kindness made her feel better almost immediately. She went to give it back to him but he shook his head. Instead he handed her the two leaves and thread of root which were all that remained of Grace's plant. Martine tried to thank him but he had already turned away and seemed to be absorbed in his book.

As the bus sped along the highway and the savannah gave way to the sharp-edged mountains and mist-wreathed forest cabins of the wintry Cape landscape, Martine tried to make head or tail of the events of the past eight hours. First the image on the cave wall and now Grace with the incomprehensible warning about a 'boat fence'. What *was* she talking about? And why would she give Martine a plant for a present?

She opened her hand and studied the scrap of green. The thin leaves oozed a milky sap where they'd been torn. With the plant destroyed there didn't seem much point in keeping them, but she couldn't bear the thought of throwing away a gift from Grace. She wrapped the leaves in Ben's bandana and found a space for them in her survival kit. The waterproof pouch had been a gift from Tendai for helping him find two missing leopard cubs. She planned to keep it around her waist for the duration of the school trip. She knew she'd probably be teased about it, but she'd made up her mind not to care.

'Most people keep their survival kit in a drawer in their house, or in a locked box in their garage, or some other place where they're probably never going to have an emergency,' Tendai had told her. 'They think they will be able to see an emergency coming. Unfortunately, that almost never happens. Keep your survival kit with you for when you most need it, little one – when you need to survive.'

The Zulu had helped her pick out what to take on this particular trip. As well as her pink Maglite torch, Martine had some matches she'd waterproofed with

43

candle wax, her Swiss Army knife, a coil of extra-strength fishing line with a hook fastened to it, three corked bottles containing Grace's special preparations for wounds, headaches and upset stomachs, a whistle, a piece of root ginger she could chew on if she felt seasick, and a tin lid with a hole in it for signalling aeroplanes.

'Surely I don't need all these things,' she'd said to Tendai. 'I mean, why would I need to signal an aeroplane?'

But Tendai replied that that was the whole point of a survival kit. You took things for every eventuality. Chances were you'd never need any of them but if you did, you wanted to be sure that all bases were covered.

By the time the cloud-scattered crags of Table Mountain came into view the kids on the bus were singing African songs, and the spirit of freedom – the feeling that by going off on a sea adventure, they were somehow playing truant – was infectious. But Martine still couldn't shake the sense that something darker lay ahead. She put a hand on her survival kit. She had a bad feeling she was going to need it.

6

In a matter of hours, Martine's misgivings had been banished by the powerful, salt-laden winds of the Cape and the sheer visual wonder of the sapphire-blue sea which pounded its shores. It helped, too, that she hadn't had a moment to think. After a tour of the penguin colonies of Simon's Town, home to South Africa's largest naval base, and a lunch of mango juice and smoked snoek paté batter-bread sandwiches, Miss Volkner had sprung a surprise on them. Before boarding the ship for the Sardine Run, they were going to 'Shark Alley' to watch tourists cage diving with Great Whites.

Shark Alley! Even the name made Martine shiver. Her gut reaction when she'd heard the news was to pretend she'd come down with food poisoning. That way, there'd be no danger of her nightmares coming true. That way, she was unlikely to end up in the choppy blue bay, encircled by sharks. Then it occurred to her that feigning illness at this stage of the journey, before they were on board the main ship, would result in her being sent back to Sawubona to face her grandmother, and even the sharks seemed preferable to that.

Barrelling over the white-capped sea a little while later on a deep-sea fishing boat named *Prowler IV,* Martine was glad she hadn't given in to her fears. She told herself they were ridiculous. It's not as if every dream she had came true. Once she'd dreamt that she'd forgotten to put on her uniform and only realized her mistake when she walked into assembly at Caracal Junior, and, to the best of her knowledge, that had never even come close to happening!

As for the image on the cave wall, well, perhaps it only meant that she'd be spending a lot of time surrounded by sharks and dolphins. Which she would. Perhaps the Bushmen had simply neglected to draw in the boat. Martine decided to stop fretting and enjoy the day. After all, what could go wrong? Safety checks on *Prowler IV* had been stringent. Stinging pellets of spray peppered her face each time the boat hit a wave, but short of being bodily hurled overboard there was very little chance of her ending up in the sea.

Geyser Rock was home to a colony of around 40,000 Cape fur seals and several hundred Jackass penguins. The seals flopped around the rocks, barking and moaning and posing for pictures, their whiskered snouts turning this way and that. Their bodies shone like bronze in the pale sunshine.

'Gourmet food for sharks,' joked Greg, *Prowler*'s skipper, a freckled South African with a bushy ginger beard. 'This is like restaurant row for Great Whites.'

Martine felt a twinge of sadness at the thought, but she understood that, if too many seals were competing for space, mates and food, it would devastate their colony. The seals needed the sharks as much as the sharks needed the seals.

As a result of the feast available to them, huge numbers of Great Whites congregated in the shallow channel between Dyer and Geyser Islands, and tourists came from all over the world to cage dive with them. Martine wasn't too sure what cage diving involved, but Greg explained that it provided an opportunity for everyone from nature lovers to adrenalin junkies to get up close and personal with the killers of the deep. There were different ways of doing it, but one of the most common was to use a cage made from galvanized steel mesh, 12mm thick. Three or four people climbed inside and the cage was lowered into the midst of feeding sharks, often only a metre or so beneath the surface.

Conservationists, Greg said, were divided over cage-diving. Some thought that it altered the behaviour of sharks, increasing the risk of them attacking humans close to beaches, but others, like Greg, who was passionate about sharks, hoped that by showing sharks in their natural habitat, more people would realize how incredible they were. Movies like *Jaws* had given them a bad name, but some sharks ate only plankton and it was rare for even Great Whites to prey on humans. Most shark attacks happened when sharks mistook surfers or swimmers for seals or fish.

Greg broke off his talk to manoeuvre *Prowler* alongside a smaller boat which was already moored in Shark Alley. There were ten tourists on the deck – three Japanese businessmen, two Germans, and a party of friendly, talkative Americans, all of whom had film star teeth. They'd spent the morning touring the islands and were very cheerful. They came aboard *Prowler* – which was now pretty crowded – and drank mugs of coffee and *rooibos*, the Afrikaans name for red bush tea, to fortify them for the cage diving experience. Martine sat chatting to Norm and Mary Weston, a couple from Florida, who were on a vacation to celebrate Norm's retirement from the staid world of vacuum cleaner sales.

'We're making it our mission to do all of the things we were too chicken or too poor to do when we were young,' Mary told Martine with a wink. 'Norm said, 'Why don't we go swimming with sharks?' And I said, 'I tell you what, darling, I'll let you swim with sharks if you let me go bungy jumping and whitewater rafting.' So we made a deal!'

Martine enjoyed talking to them and admired their spirit of adventure, but when Norm donned the thick wetsuit, boots and gloves which would protect him from the freezing temperatures of the winter water, she could tell that behind the bravado Mary was extremely anxious. The sun had been swallowed by a bank of woolly cloud and the sea was more grey than navy. It did not look inviting.

Greg, meanwhile, was busy pouring 'chum', a mixture of ground-up fish heads and other foul-smelling, bloody ingredients, guaranteed to lure sharks to the boat, into the sea. He helped Norm and three other men into the cage, and they gasped and whooped as trickles of seawater made contact with their skin. Once the sharks appeared, the tourists would be lowered beneath the surface and would breathe through hoses fed with air from the boat. Behind his goggles, Norm's face was alight with anticipation. He looked twenty years younger than his sixty-five years.

'Over there!' Scott Henderson shouted, and everyone rushed to his side of the boat, where a swishing black shadow was rising slowly from the deep. It was so enormous that Martine thought at first it was a whale, but as it neared the surface the unmistakable outline of a shark became visible. Without warning, it burst from the sea. The children and tourists reeled back. For one terrifying moment it hung in the air, so close to the boat it seemed it would land in it, and Martine saw at close range its flat grey snout, corpse-like eyes and crooked rows of needle teeth. Then it belly-flopped back into the ocean, sending a gruesome shower of chum and icy water their way.

Other Great Whites quickly joined it and soon there were as many as eighteen sharks surrounding the boat. Their fearsome jaws snapped at the fish-heads floating close to the cages. Martine could make out Norm, secure behind the steel mesh, snapping away with his underwater camera.

All at once, he stopped taking photographs and became agitated. There seemed to be a problem with his air hose. The boat assistant ran to start the machinery to raise the cage and Greg rushed to help Norm. Even before the skipper reached him, Norm had opened the lid of the cage and was attempting to clamber out.

'Slow down, Norm,' warned Greg, leaning out over the water. 'The sharks are in a feeding frenzy. You'll be okay but you need to let me help you.'

Norm smiled bravely. He put a foot on the edge of the cage and reached for Greg's freckled hand . . .

Later, when Martine tried to piece together the events of that afternoon, the thing that struck her was that it was true about accidents happening in slow motion. In reality, obviously, they took place in a split second, but that wasn't how they felt at the time. One moment

to find something its own size to terrorize or, better still, to consider a diet of plankton.

The shark's head dipped beneath the surface. The assistant threw the boathook, but it fell wide and drifted away on the current.

'STOP!' Martine yelled at the shark in her head. 'STOP!'

But the Great White was already in motion. It was like a torpedo, sleek and deadly, shooting towards the stricken man. As it approached, its jaws stretched wide and its rows of serrated teeth were plainly visible. In seconds, Norm would be missing an arm, his head or even his torso.

'STOP!' Martine yelled silently.

The shark veered away with an irritable flick of its tail. It vanished into the camouflage of the sea. The waves created by its passing shoved Norm hard against the side of the boat, where willing hands hauled him from the water.

Mary fell on him with kisses and cries of thanks. 'When you said you wanted to swim with sharks, I didn't think you meant you'd be doing it outside the cage!' she scolded her husband in a trembling voice, but it was said with humour and a lot of love.

A warm glow spread through Martine. She gave an involuntary cheer, but nobody noticed in the general bedlam. Everyone was talking at once as they tried to work out why the shark had changed course.

'At the last second it figured out that you weren't a seal, Norm,' reasoned a mightily relieved Greg, as he rushed about getting hot towels and sweet tea for his shaken client. 'Humans are just not natural prey for sharks.'

'Well, I sure am glad about that,' Norm said as the colour returned to his cheeks. 'Now, at least, I get to dine out on the story.'

In midst of all the chaos, something made Martine look up. While everyone else on the boat was focussed on the Westons' reunion, Ben, sitting cross-legged on the roof of *Prowler*'s cabin, was focussed on her. He was smiling.

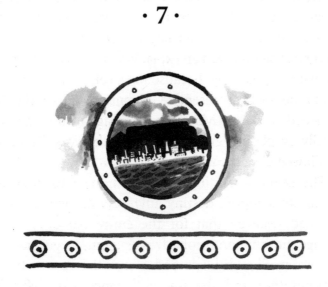

7

The following morning Martine lay on her stomach on her bunk in the *Sea Kestrel* watching a porthole-shaped dawn divide the ocean into sections of pink, apricot and blue. There was not a trace of land on the horizon. At some point during the night, Africa had slid away, taking Sawubona, Jemmy, and Martine's only connection to a home of any kind, away with it. She was adrift once more, as she had been after her parents' death. A stranger in a strange, watery wilderness, unsure of what lay ahead.

And how did she feel about that?

Well, so far, much better than she'd expected.

Overnight her mood had lifted. It was reassuring to know that the shark encounter predicted by both her dreams and the cave paintings was over, especially because it had all ended happily. It was Norm in the pictures. She even had an explanation of sorts for Grace's 'boat-fence' warning, because the steel mesh of the cage could be said to resemble a fence. The sharks had returned to haunt Martine's sleep again, but that was hardly surprising given that she'd almost seen a man swallowed alive by one!

The important thing was, she didn't have to worry about sidestepping destiny anymore, particularly since she had resolved that for the entire ten days of the voyage, nothing and nobody was going to get her into the water. She still felt bad about the row with her grandmother and she was still concerned about her future at Sawubona – life without Jemmy wasn't worth contemplating – but with no way of communicating with anyone (Miss Volkner had banned mobile phones on the ship because she wanted the class to 'lose themselves in nature'), there was nothing she could do about it until she returned to Cape Town.

To help them recover from the trauma of Shark Alley, Miss Volkner and Mr Manning, the conservationist accompanying them on their voyage, had taken the class for a seafood dinner at a harbourfront restaurant in Simon's Town. Afterwards, they'd walked through the pretty, historic streets to the docks and there she was – the *Sea Kestrel* – all lit up like some magical cruise-liner. Boarding under the moth-swirling harbour lights, with the seaweedy air teasing her nostrils, Martine had begun to appreciate how fortunate she was. She'd caught Ben's eye and it was obvious that he felt the same way.

There were twenty clean but basic cabins on the ship, with two bunks apiece. Martine was sharing a cabin with Sherilyn Meyer, a close friend of Lucy's. Sherilyn was nice enough, but a bit helpless. She had a phobia about all creatures with more than two legs. Before getting into her bunk that first night, she'd made Martine crawl around the floor checking for spiders. Martine hadn't really minded because Sherilyn's other concern – that she might get seasick – meant that Martine got to have the top bunk she was coveting, but she was thankful when the South African girl was at last satisfied the cabin was a bug-free zone, and she was able to climb between the sheets and fall into an exhausted sleep.

It had been a very, very long day.

When the red ball of sun freed itself from the smoky blue ocean, Martine slipped carefully off her bunk, showered as quietly as she could manage and went in search of sustenance. It was still early and, apart from a couple of crew smoking outside the engine room, there was nobody about. She passed a galley hatch, from which copious quantities of steam and the smell of frying bacon issued.

'Ah, a hungry sailor!' said a voice. Its owner sounded

as if he gargled regularly with beach sand. 'Step this way for an Indian Ocean breakfast!'

Martine squinted between the stainless steel shelves and dangling copper pots and saw a lively African face. A hand came out and gripped hers. 'Alberto,' said the gravelly voice. 'How do you do, Miss Martine?'

'Uhh, good morning, Alberto,' responded Martine. 'I'm very well, thank you. Have we met before?'

Alberto indicated that she should enter the galley through the main door. Martine walked into a cooking area where a diminutive African with a white cap of hair and remarkable, wrinkle-free skin was juggling sizzling pans of bacon, spiced potatoes and eggs with octopus-like dexterity. Without pausing to consult her, he lifted Martine with his small, strong hands and sat her on one of the stainless steel benches. A mug of milky coffee came her way, followed by a bacon and fried banana roll. It was not a combination of flavours that Martine had ever considered, but the crispy bacon combined with the caramel taste of bananas fried in butter was addictive. No sooner had she eaten one than she wanted another.

'Are you Mozambican?' she asked the chef in between mouthfuls. 'What tribe are you from?'

'I am Tsonga,' Alberto replied at last. 'The Tsonga are island people, living mainly in the Bazaruto Archipelago off the coast of Mozambique. And you are the girl in the story, no? The one who can ride a white giraffe.'

Martine could never get over how far news travelled on the 'bush telegraph'. African tribes and big, extended families had spent generations communicating with one another across vast swathes of savannah, desert or mountain ranges, and their conversations seemed to travel almost on the wind. Then again, several newspapers had carried photographs of her and Jemmy, so it was possible Alberto had simply read about her and might never have heard of the Zulu myth.

She took another bite of her bacon and banana roll, savoured it, and then said evasively, 'What do African islands look like, Alberto? Do they have thick bush on them and thorn trees, or are they white with palm trees?' She was thinking of the island calendar in Grace's living room which showed the Caribbean home of her father and his ancestors.

'All I know is that when I return from a long voyage and I see my home island, Benguerra, my eyes feel peaceful,' Alberto replied.

Martine understood what he meant. She experienced the same sensation whenever she passed through the gates of Sawubona. But the Bazaruto Archipelago was nothing like the golden waving grassland, thickets of acacia, and herds of zebra and elephant in the place that made her own eyes feel peaceful. Alberto conjured up images of palm-fringed islands scattered, like snowy teardrops, across a turquoise lagoon. In centuries past, he said, when it was the bountiful Southern tip of the trading routes of Arabia, the Queen of Sheba had made the islands her personal playground.

Martine knew nothing about the Queen of Sheba and didn't like to appear ignorant by asking where Sheba was or if, in fact, she had ruled over it. But it turned out that she wasn't the only one who was unclear about the queen's origins. Alberto said that, while most Africans believed the ancient kingdom of Sheba to have been close to the horn of Africa, where Eritrea and Ethiopia were now, others were convinced it was in the Yemen in Arabia.

Martine liked the notion that the queen was African royalty, and pictured her as a striking ebony woman with the high cheekbones that occurred among the tribes of north-east African nations. She'd have been dressed in robes edged with precious jewels, and seated on a throne mounted on the prow of a great sailing ship. In between visiting King Solomon to test his wisdom, as she was reported to have done in Biblical times, she'd have floated around the Bazaruto Islands, eating oysters and pink lobsters and buying gold.

The Portuguese came next, in the 16th century. Alberto rolled his eyes a little when he talked of them and it was clear that he was not a fan of the way they had colonized his country, gobbling land, setting up ivory trading posts and penal colonies, and making a fortune harvesting the oyster beds around the Bazaruto Islands, which yielded some of the creamiest pearls on earth. Legend had it that the captains of ships sent to transport precious cargoes of gold, pearls and beads, hurled the odd casket overboard, in locations marked on secret maps, in the hope that they might one day be able to return for them. And that since they rarely did, treasures beyond imagining lay buried under the seas around the islands.

Martine was watching Norm balance on the edge of the cage like a black-winged crane, reaching for Greg's hand; the next, time had slowed to a crawl and she was watching as the American, unsteady from lack of oxygen, missed Greg's fingers and fell backwards into the churning grey sea.

The wheeling gulls matched Mary's screams.

Norm landed with a terrific splash, temporarily scattering the sharks. The scene took on a surreal quality. It didn't seem possible that the smiling man with whom Martine been sharing coffee and biscuits barely half an hour earlier was now flailing about in the bloody water, fighting for his life. But this was no movie. The largest of the Great Whites, a prize specimen of about twenty-two feet – Greg had told them that it probably weighed close to 7,000lbs – had already changed direction and was on its way back to see if Norm was edible. The boat was a madhouse, with Greg appealing for calm while his assistant hung over the edge with a boathook. He planned to bash the shark on the nose, its most sensitive part, if it came within range.

The menacing shadow circled Norm twice. The pinched snout of the shark poked above the water and its mouth opened briefly as if it were testing to see how much of him it could bite off in one go. It was then that Martine seized her chance. She focussed her green eyes on the shark's sunken grey ones, summoned all the furious energy she could muster and directed it at the shark in a conscious stream, the way she'd once done with a rottweiler dog. She willed it to leave Norm alone,

Modern life on Benguerra seemed to consist of prawn feasts and trees laden with cashew nuts, marulas and monkey oranges. Alberto talked proudly of how the Tsonga had remained more or less untouched by the decades of invaders, civil war and strife which had affected the rest of Mozambique.

'During the war, we would sit under the palms on our islands and watch the flashes of rocket fire on the mainland light up the night skies, and our hearts would break for our brothers and sisters. Even now, we hear stories of hunger, disease and murder in the cities, but we know nothing of such things on Benguerra. If today you leave your camera on the beach, tomorrow somebody will find it and bring it to you. The smallest children can walk anywhere on the island by themselves. We don't have locks on our doors. We say to our neighbours, "Come, everything we have is yours." '

To Martine, it sounded like paradise, although like all paradises it had its little drawbacks. In the summer months, the heat and malaria-carrying mosquitoes were torture, and Alberto's home island was famous for having enormous numbers of snakes.

'These are small things,' the chef said. 'Truly we are blessed to live in such a wonderful place. But you know, even special places can change. With the islands becoming so popular, many outsiders are coming in, and some of our young people are moving out. They get tired of the old ways and want to move to the towns, where they think they will find more money and more fun.'

'I wish *we* were going to the Bazaruto Islands,' Martine

said. 'We're only going as far as Inhambane, in the south of Mozambique, where we're supposed to help count the population of dugongs, and then we're returning to Cape Town.'

Alberto gave a throaty laugh, revealing a little red gemstone set in one of his front teeth. It flashed like fire in the galley lights. 'That is true,' he said. 'We are not going to Bazaruto. But you never know in this life.'

8

The one thing the class had been told over and over was that the Sardine Run was unpredictable. It was a natural phenomenon and natural phenomena were not in the habit of organizing their timetables to suit school trips, or reporters with deadlines, or tourists on expensive Sardine Run package tours. The sardines responded to subtle changes in water temperature and if the temperature didn't spur them to make a move, sometimes they didn't 'run' at all. Every day Mr Manning radioed the Sharks Board in KwaZulu-Natal to check if there were any sightings, and every day he came away disappointed.

His disappointment was nothing compared to that of the children. They'd heard so much about the Sardine Run that their expectations were sky high. The majority of them had not bothered to read Miss Volkner's notes on the voyage and had imagined themselves on a cruise ship like the famous *QE2*, with sun-loungers and jacuzzis, and plenty of time to nap beside the pool in their swimwear. Even those who had glanced through the notes had thought of the trip as a vacation from schoolwork.

The reality was a little different. The *Sea Kestrel* had more in common with a fishing trawler than a luxury liner. There were no sun-loungers, drinks with umbrellas in them, seafood buffets, or other cruise ship luxuries. There were bare boards and bare essentials only. As for getting a holiday, the children found that the opposite was the case. Caracal Junior was an eco-school, which meant that there was a strong emphasis on the environment in lessons, and Miss Volkner and Mr Manning were determined that not a moment of the ten-day voyage would be wasted.

From morning till night, the class were kept busy with conservation projects. They identified migrating sea birds, or collected jars of sea water and examined their contents under microscopes for traces of things like phyloplankton.

'Phyloplankton is phosphorescent,' explained Mr Manning. 'That means it glows in the dark. It looks like fairy floss under the moonlight. Dolphins and whales swim through it and it coats their bodies like a film. If you see them playing in the waves at night, it looks as if they're outlined in silver.'

Martine was so entranced by this that she spent the next few evenings running back and forth on the deck to check if there were any fairy-flossed dolphins leaping alongside the ship, but none appeared.

She cornered Mr Manning one afternoon to ask him why dolphins and whales beached themselves. Mr Manning was not a man who did anything speedily and it took him a while to answer. He removed his spectacles, which had a chipped lens and a broken arm he had mended himself with yellow insulation tape, and wiped sea-spray off the lenses.

'To be honest, Martine,' he said, 'it's a bit of a mystery. Sometimes it has an obvious cause, such as dolphins being wounded by fishing gear, or bite wounds from sharks, or being ill. But when large numbers of dolphins and whales are involved it's not that simple. Alberto was telling me that, in the Bazaruto Islands, dolphins have beached themselves on the thirteenth day of each of the past three months. Isn't that peculiar? Some Tsonga believe that it's because the dolphins have become drunk on rainwater, and around the world other cultures have their own ideas. But many scientists are now coming round to the theory that one of the main causes is sonar.'

'Sonar? You mean the thing ships use to communicate with each other?'

'Exactly. SOund Navigation and Ranging is its full name. It was invented in 1906 by a man called Lewis Nixon as a way of detecting icebergs, and then modified by a French physicist and a Russian engineer for use in detecting submarines during the First World War. These days, of course, sonar is used extensively by the Navy for military purposes, and many other people and organizations for all sorts of other things. For instance, fishermen use it to find shoals of fish.'

The *Sea Kestrel* was steaming through the waves in response to a supposed Sardine Run sighting, and Martine and Mr Manning moved back from the railings to avoid the flying spray. 'I don't understand,' said Martine. 'Why would that cause dolphins and whales to want to escape the sea?'

'Ah, well, you see whales and dolphins use a kind of sonar to locate prey and find their way around the oceans. It's known as echolocation. Scientists fear that the Low-Frequency Active (LFA) sonar used by the Navy disorientates and confuses them. It sweeps the ocean like a sort of floodlight and the sound it gives off can carry up to 100 miles and be as loud as a fighter jet at take-off. In some cases, it can cause whales to surface too quickly, leading to a fatal condition similar to the bends in human beings. They get gas bubbles in their organs. Their brains bleed.

'Sometimes the sonar is so deafening that it bursts their ear drums. A few years ago, LFA testing in the Bahamas was found to be responsible for the stranding of sixteen whales, seven of which were found dead. There have been numerous similar incidents across the planet, often when there have been naval exercises in the area. The total number of cases runs into thousands.

300 hundred dolphins in Zanzibar, 130 pilot whales in Tasmania, 68 dolphins in Florida . . . '

He polished his glasses again. 'This is not a very cheerful subject, is it? Why are you so interested in it, anyway? Have you seen any beached dolphins?'

Martine gave him an angelic smile. She was not about to tell the conservationist about her experience with the dolphin in Cape Town. 'I just love dolphins.'

'Then I'll tell you some nice things about them,' Mr Manning said. 'Their pointed snout is called a rostrum. Did you know that? And have you heard that dolphins know each other's names? Isn't that wonderful! Each one of them has its own signature whistle.'

Martine was intrigued but before she could ask another question, a cry went up, 'The Sardine Run! We've found the Sardine Run!'

Every person not engaged in the sailing of the ship converged on the starboard edge, but there were no sardines to be seen. Instead it was as if the *Sea Kestrel* was entering a bizarre weather system. Oddly-shaped clouds were scudding across the sky and tufts of spray were kicking up randomly.

'This is the Sardine Run?' said Luke, distinctly unimpressed. 'This is what we've come all this way for? The sardines aren't even visible.'

'Be patient,' counselled Mr Manning. 'Wait till we get up close.'

'Mind if I take a nap?' Luke said under his breath, and Lucy sniggered.

Martine stayed staring hopefully ahead, watching for dolphins. The ship forged through the waves. At length, the curious clouds resolved themselves into birds – hundreds and hundreds of Cape gannets and cormorants – all dive-bombing the sea. Then she spotted the sardines. Seen from above, they looked like an immense silver oil-slick. So dense was the shoal and so closely did the flashing fish swim together that it was as if they were being directed by an invisible conductor. A whale sliced slowly through the middle of the silver symphony, chomping sardines as it went.

The dolphins came next, several hundred of them. They converged on the shoal at blinding speed and worked like sheepdogs to corral a mass of sardines into a tight ball, on which they proceeded to gorge themselves. 'That's what's known as a "baitball",' explained Mr Manning, who was practically levitating he was so excited.

The children were awestruck. Even Luke and Lucy were silent with wonder. Martine realized that her mouth was hanging open.

The *Sea Kestrel* anchored within sight of the beach, although the sand could not be seen for the crowds pouring down to the water. As the sardine shoal entered the shallows, the human tide tore into the sea, shouting and squealing, to fight over the feast with the birds.

There were children with plastic buckets, men with nets, pots, pans and even wheelbarrows, and women scooping sardines into the skirts of their dresses and handbags. It was pure frenzy.

Then, just as suddenly as it had started, it was over. The sardine shoal dropped out of sight and the whirling birds moved on. Only the dolphins remained, sated now but still milling around the ship as if they were waiting for something.

'Martine,' said Mr Manning, 'could you do me a favour and fetch my binoculars from the prow? I left them on the bench close to where we were talking.'

Martine was too overwhelmed to reply but she nodded and wandered unsteadily towards the front of the ship, trailing her fingers along the rails. She was halfway there when she noticed that some thirty dolphins had separated from the pod, and were moving along the side of the *Sea Kestrel* in the same direction she was. When she reached the prow, they congregated below her. The ship was at anchor, so Martine put the binoculars to her eyes and leaned over the rail to study them. She wondered what they were up to.

The dolphins were fuzzy through the lenses of the binoculars, but she adjusted the focus and their grey faces and pink mouths popped into view. Every one of their faces was turned upwards, and they were all clicking and whistling at once. Martine took the glasses from her eyes to see who or what they were chattering to, but no one was there. They appeared to be talking to her!

'What do you want?' Martine called down to them,

68

bending over the railings. 'What are you asking me?'

Aware that she was keeping Mr Manning waiting, she began to stroll slowly back to the other end of the ship, keeping her eyes on the dolphins. To her amazement, they followed her again. She was so absorbed that she didn't see Mr Manning until she slammed into him. Several of her classmates were gathered around him, staring at her with envious disbelief.

'Extraordinary!' Mr Manning said. 'This is my eighth Sardine Run and I've never seen anything like it. It's almost as if you were a sort of dolphin Pied Piper. I mean, why would they follow you like that?'

Out of the corner of her eye, Martine saw the dolphins slip beneath the sea's rocking blue surface.

'I think it was coincidence,' she told him. 'There were some fish jumping around the prow and the dolphins just happened to go there at the same time as I went to get the binoculars. Then they returned at the same time too.'

'Yes,' said Mr Manning doubtfully. 'Yes, I suppose that must be it.'

9

Late afternoon on their fifth day at sea, the wind began to make a keening noise like a pack of wolves. By dinner time, every heave of the ship sent crockery and knives and forks smashing and clashing, and orange fish soup stains were splattered across the tablecloths. It was hard to walk, let alone keep the food which had gone down from coming up again, and not everybody made it through the meal. Sherilyn was the first to go, triggering an exodus as she raced green-faced for the exit, after the rolling ship and the discovery of a squid eye at the bottom of her bowl proved too much for her.

Soon there were only a handful of children at the

tables. Above their heads, light bulbs tinkled in their holders and misshapen monster shadows chased one another around the walls. Martine, who felt fine, didn't fancy being trapped in a cabin with a seasick Sherilyn, nor did she want to hang around the recreation room where Claudius could be heard regaling anyone who would listen with stories about the time his family, who owned an ocean-going yacht which had once belonged to a Greek billionaire, had sailed through a hurricane in the Cayman Islands, 'The waves were sixty feet high! My father said, "Son, your hand's steadier than mine, so you take the wheel while I plot a course to keep us ahead of the storm's eye…" '

Grimacing, Martine ducked out of the door and turned left along the swaying corridor to the galley. She was just in time to see Ben disappearing down the stairs to the engine room, and she smiled to herself. This had become their ritual. Every evening after dinner, when everyone else was watching DVDs or playing board games, she and Ben were in separate parts of the ship talking to the crew.

Ben's father was a sailor and Ben adored boats and anything to do with the sea, so Martine knew that he'd be learning how the *Sea Kestrel* worked. She, meanwhile, had become firm friends with Alberto, bonding over daily breakfasts of bacon and banana rolls and after-dinner treats of crème caramel dessert or coconut cake.

On her third night on board Martine had been unable to sleep because, at dinner, Miss Volkner had told her that she absolutely had to join the rest of the class when they were snorkelling and searching for dugongs in Mozambique. She wasn't interested in excuses. After that the conversation at the table had moved on to shipwrecks and the many reasons ships sunk, so that by the time Martine reached her bunk all she could think about was the washing-machine wave engulfing her and water pouring into her nose and mouth.

She'd tossed and turned for what seemed like hours before giving up and creeping quietly out of the cabin, taking care not to rouse Sherilyn. Alberto wasn't in the galley but she'd found him up on deck, smoking and looking out over the inky sea.

'You look very troubled for one so young,' was the chef's comment.

Martine denied it at first, but after a long pause she said, 'Alberto, were you ever afraid of the ocean or even just, you know, of deep water?'

The chef smiled ruefully. 'Many times I have been scared on the dhows, the sailing boats which we use in the Bazaruto Islands. Many, many times. As a boy, especially. But my grandfather was a fisherman. One night a cyclone swept through the islands of Bazaruto, uprooting palm trees and whipping up waves as big as houses. The dhow he was on overturned, leaving him and four others in the sea, but the dolphins – *mathahi* we call them in our language – they surrounded them and protected them from the sharks. After this time I was afraid no more.'

He studied Martine kindly. 'The *Sea Kestrel* is a big, solid ship,' he said, in case she thought otherwise. 'It would take a bomb to sink her.'

They'd gone down to the galley after that and Alberto had made her a mug of malted Milo, which he'd heated in a pot on the stove. Martine had felt a bit shy because the chef was a virtual stranger and yet there she was in her pyjamas, about to tell him things she couldn't even admit to her grandmother. But she knew instinctively he wouldn't think any less of her for them.

When the hot, sweet Milo gave her courage to speak, she said, 'I don't know what's wrong with me, Alberto. At Sawubona, the game reserve where I live, I've ridden my giraffe at night with lions, hippos and buffaloes. I've almost been bitten by a Cape cobra, escaped from poachers with guns, and been in underground caves with bats. Yet I've never been as afraid of any of those things as I am of deep water. I loved the Sardine Run and I especially loved the dolphins, but I just don't feel at home on the ocean. I was okay when I thought I wouldn't have to go in the sea, but this evening Miss Volkner told me that I absolutely have to go snorkelling when we reach Mozambique, and I'm scared that something will go wrong and I'll drown because I'm a terrible swimmer. Alberto, I'm the worst swimmer in the whole school.'

'I would be afraid of a giraffe if I saw one,' Alberto replied, somewhat confusingly.

Martine was puzzled. 'Why? Giraffes are the gentlest animals in the world. They'd never dream of hurting anyone. Not unless they were trapped, or threatened, or protecting their young.'

'I'm sure you are right but I have never been close to any wild animal, apart from whales, dolphins and dugongs, and I have never been in a safari park. I would be afraid because it is all unknown. You are afraid of the sea because you don't understand it. It is not familiar to you. So you shall know about it.'

On the night of the storm, Martine sat on the stainless steel bench in the galley, swinging her legs and listening to Alberto talk about what she thought of as 'island-craft.' Tendai had taught her bushcraft – vital tips and tricks to help her understand and survive the natural laws of the African savannah, and in some ways the chef did the same for the marine environment of his homeland.

'On Benguerra,' he said, bracing his legs against the rolling of the ship, which seemed to be worsening by the minute, 'the children of fishermen learn from their earliest days to catch fish in many different ways, because their fathers believe it will teach them to know the sea's secrets and be grateful for the gifts that it provides. So they send each child out to catch his or her own pilot fish, a small fish which hitches rides with large fish like they are buses. When they find this pilot fish, they tie a fishing line around it and send it out to sea. When it attaches itself to a big fish, they reel it in, eat the big fish and set the little one to work again!'

Alberto liked to hear about life on Sawubona as well, so Martine told him about Tendai and about Grace's traditional medicine and her wonderful cooking. Alberto's local witchdoctor, a young male *sangoma*, was very different to Grace. According to the chef, he spent more time in a football shirt than a feather headdress, and had never been known to say no to a lethal moonshine called palm wine. Alberto told her a story about a villager who'd once gone to him with a skull-splitting headache. The footballing witchdoctor had started the treatment by putting a large pebble into his fire. While it was heating up, he blended herbs in a bowl made from a special wood and engraved with a cross, then added water. When the stone was red-hot he dropped it into the bowl, causing the water to boil and turn green. After making a series of tiny incisions in the man's forehead, the witchdoctor rubbed in a little of the herb potion and sent him home with the remainder in a bottle and the wooden bowl on his head.

'From that day on, no more headaches,' Alberto said with a grin.

Martine expressed what she hoped was the right amount of respectful admiration, while privately thinking that Grace was clearly a better traditional healer by miles, since her remedies were not based on hocus-pocus like putting bowls on people's heads, but had been tried and tested by all the grandmothers going back hundreds of years. She cast a critical eye over Alberto's smooth brown forehead. 'Do *you* go to the witchdoctor for headaches?' she asked.

Alberto chuckled. 'No, I prefer to take an aspirin.'

He was interrupted by a thunderbolt so ear-piercing it

sounded as if the *Sea Kestrel* had collided with an iceberg. The ship bucked wildly. Martine flew off the stainless steel bench and hit the tiles with a painful smack. A split second later, a stack of plates sailed off a shelf and shattered against the bench in the exact spot where she'd been sitting. A confetti of sharp ceramic chips showered spikily down on her head. Alberto helped her up, dusted white flecks of plate from her hair, and checked her for cuts and bruises, but he was no longer laughing.

'Miss Martine,' he said darkly, 'this is like the cyclone that nearly stole my grandfather. I have work to do to secure the galley. You must go now and stay close to your friends and your teachers.'

The ship was tossing violently and both he and Martine were holding onto the bench for support. Martine felt a mounting sense of alarm. Unbidden, the shark and dolphin cave painting came into her head. What if she'd been mistaken and the picture had not been about the Sardine Run or the incident at Shark Alley? What if the prophecy was yet to be fulfilled?

She said to Alberto, 'What makes you think this is a cyclone? Surely it's just a bad storm, and you told me that this was a big, solid ship. You told me it would take a bomb to sink her.'

Just then, the siren began to wail.

· 10 ·

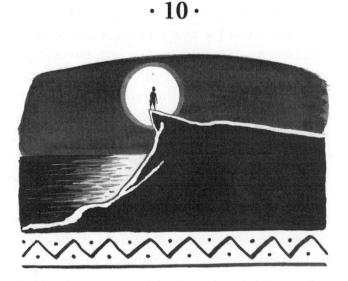

In the corridor, frightened children in puffy orange lifejackets were streaming up to the deck. Some, like Sherilyn, were a ghastly colour. They wore pyjamas with the buttons done up wrong and dressing gowns with trailing cords and one boy had on a lone leopard-print slipper. Others had flung on mismatched clothes in clashing colours and had sticking-up sleep hair. Only Lucy, immaculate in a white tracksuit with a red trim, looked as if she was on her way for a lesson at the tennis club. Most of the girls were crying.

Miss Volkner and Mr Manning were doing their best to keep everybody calm by telling them that this was nothing more than a routine safety procedure and they'd be back in their bunks in no time.

'Walk, don't run,' ordered the teacher, trying to make herself heard above the racket of the siren. 'No, Boysie, you can't bring your suitcase. You want what? Yes, you can bring Pooh Bear.'

Martine darted unnoticed through a side door. Her survival kit had been around her waist for the entire duration of the trip, as she'd promised Tendai it would be, but she'd taken it off to shower before dinner and had forgotten to put it back on again. In the event this was a real emergency, she wanted it with her.

The siren's insistent blare had shut off and the cabins were eerily quiet. Martine was reminded unpleasantly of a ship disaster film she'd watched with her parents. She took the survival kit from behind the locker where she'd hidden it and tied it securely around her waist. Then she put on a windcheater. As a sort of tribute to Grace, she'd put the forlorn remnants of her plant in a blue mineral water bottle Alberto had given her. The bottle had toppled over and was lying in a puddle on the floor. Martine wrapped the leaves in Ben's bandana again and added them to her survival kit. She felt a little silly doing it, but there was something about the wisp of plant that made her feel connected to Grace and Sawubona. The last thing she did was take off her shoes. She always felt better barefoot. She was on her way to join her classmates when she heard voices coming from the recreation room.

'But don't you think we should go up to the deck?'

Luke was saying. 'What if it's serious? What if the ship is sinking and we miss getting on the lifeboat? And anyway, won't they take a roll call?'

Claudius laughed. 'Please tell me you're kidding. You are kidding, aren't you? This is a drill, that's all it is. Or maybe it's just some teacher who knows nothing about the sea getting into a panic over a breeze and a bit of rain. This is nothing compared to some of the storms I've been through on our yacht. There's no way I'm going out there and getting drenched to the skin for nothing. I'm going to stay where it's warm and dry and watch a film.'

'Look, I'm sorry but I have to go check on Lucy,' Luke said apologetically. 'Even if it is only a drill, she'll still be scared.'

'Hey, no hard feelings,' Claudius told him. 'See you in ten minutes.'

Anxious to avoid being seen by either boy, Martine skipped nimbly up to the deck. She was almost flattened by the force of the storm which lunged at her out of the night. In seconds, her jeans were soaked through. Luke pushed past her, shielding his face from the onslaught. He leaned into the wind and headed for the prow, where the rest of the children were gathered in a dripping bunch, outlined against the torrid sky. They appeared to be receiving emergency evacuation instructions from a couple of crew members. Lucy threw her arms around her twin and handed him the lifejacket she'd been keeping for him. Even through the rain and from a distance, Martine could see how ecstatic she was to see him, and she thought how great it must be to have someone who loved you unconditionally no matter what. That made her remember Jemmy and she was glad that at least one creature on earth loved her that way.

Unconditionally.

Miss Volkner and Mr Manning emerged from the doorway behind Martine. 'You've checked every cabin?' Miss Volkner was saying. Her red curls waved madly in the wind. 'You're absolutely sure there's nobody left below deck?'

Martine wondered what had become of Claudius. As much as she disliked him, she knew she should tell Miss Volkner he was planning to stay in the rec room for the duration of the storm. But before she could say anything, the teacher let out a startled shriek, 'Martine, *where* is your lifejacket? Where are your shoes? Lord, give me strength. What are you doing here? Why aren't . . . ?'

The rest of her tirade was drowned by the screech of splitting metal. Jake Emery, who had been leaning over the edge of the ship, transfixed by the raging sea, jumped back, a horrified look on his face. A section of rail had torn loose and was swinging like a gate in the gale.

Grace's words came back to Martine. 'Beware of the boat-fence.'

The boat-fence! Of course! It was the railing around the ship. How could she have been so blind? How could she have missed something so obvious? The railing was going to be the cause of a catastrophe.

Martine started forward but Miss Volkner grabbed her by the arm. 'Oh, no you don't,' she cried. 'You're not going anywhere until you've got a lifejacket on.'

Martine tried to twist away but Miss Volkner was surprisingly strong. 'The guard rail,' Martine screamed in the direction of the kids near the prow, cupping a hand over her mouth. 'Get away from the guard rail!'

But the wind and the roaring sea swallowed her words and the only one to look her way was Ben.

The ship pitched sharply. Miss Volkner lost her balance and was forced to let go of Martine to save herself. The children near the railing went down like dominoes. Through slanting sheets of rain, Martine saw Ben start towards her. She blinked and he was gone.

She blinked again but he was definitely gone.

Concerned that he might somehow have fallen overboard, Martine leapt out of range of Miss Volkner's clutching fingers and started running along the slippery deck, ignoring her teacher's enraged shouts. The pelting rain stung her face. Beneath her feet, the ship rolled and shuddered, and foaming crests of waves shot so high above the sides of the ship they might have been tsunamis. Two sailors were untying the lifeboat. That's when the severity of the crisis really came home to Martine. If the storm didn't abate soon, she could end up living her nightmare.

She rounded the ship's funnel and stopped short. Two figures, one large and one much smaller, were wrestling in darkness, lashed by the driving rain. Claudius and Ben!

'Give it to me, you little runt,' panted Claudius as he wrenched at Ben's lifejacket, trying to pull it off by brute force.

Ben wriggled out of Claudius's desperate grip and held up a hand in a gesture of surrender. There was a faint smile on his lips. The look he gave the bigger boy spoke so many volumes that it rendered Martine, who'd been about to intervene, temporarily paralyzed. Mainly it was a look of pity. It was a look that said, 'If you want this lifejacket so much that you're prepared to do this terrible thing, you need it much more than I do.'

Then he unzipped the orange vest and handed it to Claudius.

Claudius snatched it from him without a word, pulled it on over his tubby frame, and stumbled away into the rain-swept night. Martine went up to Ben. She was sickened by what she'd seen. She wanted to rush after Claudius and pound her fists against his meaty back, or rant to Ben about how evil he was, but she knew Ben wouldn't appreciate either. So she just said, 'Don't worry, I don't have a lifejacket either,' which she knew was a bit lame because why would it be of any comfort to him that she, too, was without a safety vest?

The same thought must have occurred to him because his mouth curled up at the corners and he replied, 'Well, that's okay then!'

Another tsunami-like wave rose into the night, its crest glistening like shaving foam. Martine remembered that she was supposed to be trying to move everyone away from the railings. Hurriedly she told Ben about Grace's warning and together they pushed into the teeth of the gale. Their progress was slowed by the sheer volume of water swilling around their ankles.

They were within reach of their classmates when the ship dipped so steeply it seemed certain it was going to upend. One moment Martine was straining to stay upright on the waterlogged deck, the next, the deck wasn't there. The momentum of their run carried her and Ben helplessly forwards and they collided with the tangle of bodies. There was a screech of tearing metal and the entire rail gave way. Next time Martine looked, some of the children didn't seem to be there any more.

Before she could fully comprehend what was happening the deck was dropping away again. Once more Martine had the feeling that time had slowed to a crawl. First she grabbed at a steel post in a bid to save herself. It came away in her hand. Secondly she took in that the din on the boat – the slashing rain, the roaring sea, the screams and yells – was hurting her ears. Finally, Martine noticed that the two girls in front of her, the last line of resistance between her and the witches' cauldron of ocean, had lost their grip on the slippery edge and were on their way overboard.

Then time speeded up again and she was plunging after them, tumbling headfirst into the darkness, and the seething, sucking sea was reaching up to claim her.

11

*C*oncrete. That's what went through Martine's mind. When you hit water from a great height, it feels like concrete. It almost winded her. The icy shock of it blasted the remaining air from her lungs and before she knew it she was spinning helplessly into the jet-black deep, dropping like a human anchor until she was sure she'd hit the ocean floor, 10,000 leagues under the sea. Then, just as suddenly she was shooting up again, flailing, spitting saltwater, gasping for breath.

Already, the ship was further away than she could ever have believed was possible, but it was still within reach. She could see people scurrying around the deck. They were throwing lines and lowering a lifeboat. A weaving searchlight illuminated pale heads bobbing in the surrounding sea. Martine struck out in their direction but her clothes and the survival kit weighed her down and restricted her movements, and she could have been a cork on a rapid for all the impression her efforts made on the treacle-black waves. She went to unbuckle the pouch but something stopped her. 'Keep your survival kit with you for when you most need it, little one,' Tendai had told her, 'when you need it to survive.' He hadn't said anything about what to do if the kit supposed to save you was dragging you down to the bottom of the sea, but there was no denying that this was a survival situation if ever there was one.

Martine was panic-stricken. She yelled for help, but it was a feeble yell because she was beyond the arc of the searchlights and she knew with nauseating certainty that they wouldn't be able hear her on deck; that if she couldn't reach the boat before the waves obscured her, she'd be left alone in the raging ocean in the middle of the night, waiting to drown or be eaten by sharks.

Fear lent her energy. She started to swim again. To distract herself, she did her best to imagine she was competing in the school gala, but that only reminded her of how she always came last. So she put her head down and concentrated instead on doing one stroke at a time. When she judged she must be nearing the lifeboat, she stopped and trod water. Her chest constricted with shock. The ship was a fast-shrinking square of light on the horizon! Martine wiped the salt water from her eyes and, when a swell lifted her up again, squinted into the darkness. But there was no mistake. The current and the huge waves had swept her away. At least a mile lay between her and any hope of rescue. She was on her own.

Battling to stay afloat, Martine started to cry. Breaking down went against everything she knew about survival, the most crucial part of which was staying calm and not giving up, but she couldn't help it. It would take a miracle to save her now. Already, she was completely exhausted. She'd swallowed gallons of seawater and she was so cold she didn't know which was going to get her first, hypothermia or the sharks that lurked in the depths below. She could imagine them circling in preparation for charging at her the way the Great White had hurtled at Norm in Shark Alley, their deep-set, dead eyes on her flapping white limbs. She tried to paddle more slowly and to tuck her legs up, to minimise the area of flesh they had to attack, but all that happened was that she sank.

Terrified, she clawed her way to the surface. She was almost there when there was an explosion of bubbles and a shining streak passed her – a sort of oceanic shooting star. Then it swooped the other way. Martine tried to focus, to see it through the darkness and rain, but the whale-tail strength of the waves shoved her back and forth and she caught only glimpses of a long, swiftly moving shape, glowing with some unearthly light.

Instinct told Martine that if she could only reach the shining thing it would mean survival. But she kept sinking. No matter how hard she struggled, it stayed tantalizingly out of reach. And with every passing second the chill was numbing her limbs, making the sea seem heavy, as if she was swimming through snow. She was so tired that she knew she wouldn't be able to fight for much longer. Soon she'd have to stop paddling and then . . .

The edges of Martine's vision wavered and darkness closed in.

It was Cornwall she remembered first. A spring day on Porthmeor Beach in St Ives, before the summer madness when the tourists came. Martine had been standing on the apricot sand, reaching for a honeycomb ice cream mum had bought her, when a fat seagull had swooped down and snatched it. But her dismay had quickly turned to laughter. While the seagull was gloating over its spoils on a nearby rooftop – sending ear-piercing screeches in their direction – another seagull had reached over and swallowed the cone in a single gulp! By then Martine and her dad had decided that it was too chilly for ice cream anyway, so the three of them had spent the rest of the afternoon scoffing warm scones heaped with strawberry jam and clotted cream in a cosy harbour café, watching the tide spill in around the rainbow-painted fishing boats.

Martine remembered it as a day of perfect happiness.

Other memories followed, flickering through her head like a well-loved home movie. There was the magical night on the game reserve when she'd woken from a dead faint to find the white giraffe towering over her, his coat shimmering like sun on snow, his silver patches tinged with cinnamon; the exhilaration she'd felt the first time she rode him – the way they'd swept across the moonlit savannah, Jemmy galloping with a rocking-horse stride.

Next, and as vividly as if it was happening then, Martine felt electricity crackle through her just as it had when Grace placed a hand on her forehead on the day she arrived in Africa. 'The gift can be a blessing or a curse,' the *sangoma* had warned her. 'Make your decisions wisely.'

The scene changed and Martine relived the horror of the fire and the last time she saw her parents, when her father had hugged her goodnight and told her he loved her. She'd been about to go into her bedroom when he'd said, 'You have to trust, Martine. Everything happens for a reason.' And afterwards she'd thought how odd it was that he should say it then, at that precise moment.

Last – and as if she was watching from above – she saw herself as a baby. She was in her mother's arms in the living room at Sawubona. Mum was holding her up to the window so she could glimpse the animals – lions beside zebras, leopards beside springbok, baboons beside warthogs – lined up along the game fence, their eyes trained on the house. 'See that, beautiful girl,' Veronica murmured. 'That's your destiny.'

Then, almost imperceptibly, she had added, 'But not if I can stop it.'

Gradually Martine became aware that she was being raised to the surface of the sea by something immensely strong and yet infinitely gentle, like angels' wings. A blast of stormy air hit her face and shocked her back to life, and then she was coughing up seawater and sucking oxygen into her burning lungs. She was draped across something solid and slippery. For a minute she lay there, grateful for the opportunity to rest and breathe and be partially out of the freezing water. Then the solid thing moved. Martine, who'd been idly speculating she had happened upon a piece of floating wreckage or, miracle of miracles, the lifeboat, nearly passed out with fright. She struggled upright. The clouds cleared from her vision and she realized that she was holding onto a large dorsal fin.

A shark! She was sitting on a shark!

Then a nose poked above the water and emitted a few clicks and squeaks, and Martine was filled with an intense relief. In spite of her predicament, she laughed out loud. She'd been rescued by a dolphin. All of a sudden it didn't seem so bad that she was in the middle of the ocean in the middle of the night, with the ship long gone. She wasn't sure what was going to become of her now, but whatever it was it had to be better than being snacked on by sharks.

Even as she was congratulating herself on this piece of good fortune, a movement in the blue-black water caught Martine's eye. A dorsal fin cruised slowly by. She tried to see it clearly. Surely it was another dolphin? Surely it was a friend, come to join her saviour? But the dorsal fin began to circle and soon it was joined by a second fin and a third, fourth, fifth and sixth. In a matter of minutes, she and the dolphin were ring-fenced in a deadly shark corral. Martine was already shaking with cold and exertion, but now she began to shiver so violently at the thought that she might, after all, be torn apart in a feeding frenzy of Great Whites (Greg's talk about their many good qualities had failed to reassure her) that she was worried she might slip off the dolphin. And anyway, what was to prevent her newfound friend from darting away to save itself, abandoning her to her fate? But the dolphin stayed with her, although it made squeaks of alarm at the encroaching sharks.

Suddenly the sharks melted away. Nothing happened for a moment and then, over the sighing of the sea, Martine heard a tremendous splashing. What she saw next took her breath away. Through the wild waves came what must have been 100 dolphins, their silhouettes outlined in silver. They were leaping, dancing and cavorting, and their silvery arcs, freeze-framed against the midnight ocean and the scudding storm clouds, were beyond beautiful. Martine sat perfectly still, awed by the spectacle. As they drew nearer, she could hear them communicating with one another and it sounded to her like music; like singing. And whether or not it was her imagination, she fancied they were singing in Xhosa, because their clicks were not dissimilar to the lovely clicks made by African singers she'd heard. And that, strangely, calmed her and made her feel that somehow, some way, she'd be all right.

The dolphins surrounded Martine in their dozens and opened their smiling mouths and squeaked and whistled, almost as if they were greeting her. That was amazing enough, especially because they allowed her to reach down and stroke their satin skins, but then Martine noticed that several of the dolphins were transporting passengers. The other kids! Most seemed barely conscious. A couple cast desperate glances in her direction, blinked in acknowledgement and resumed their frozen postures on the dolphins' backs, sobbing quietly.

Martine counted five figures, but as far as she could tell, Ben wasn't among them. What if he hadn't been saved? What if he was lost at sea? What if he was gone forever? She tried to imagine life without the boy who, in the shortest possible time, had come to mean so much to her, and was taken aback by the pain that suddenly speared her heart. After all, it's not as if she really *knew* him. Ben wasn't someone it was easy to get to know. She always had the impression that he was watching the world from some peaceful place inside himself.

Martine was so busy agonizing over Ben and whether or not she could have interpreted Grace's clue sooner and prevented the whole disaster that she didn't notice a new dolphin entering the ranks of those around her until it actually nudged her foot. Ben was slumped on its back. By the look of him, he was drowned, or very close to it.

'Ben!' cried Martine hysterically. 'Ben, wake up! Oh, please be alive. Please be alive.'

When he didn't respond, she shook him hard. She was so afraid that this was to be her fate – to lose everyone she ever cared about – that she forgot everything she knew about First Aid. Ben sat up, startled, his eyes glazed. She could see him trying to make sense of the scene around him. Perhaps he, like her, had dreamed he was somewhere else. Slowly his expression began to register the same incredulity Martine had experienced as he took in the fact that not only was he surrounded by dolphins; he was on the back of one. Then he saw Martine herself. Wordlessly he reached for her hand. He made no effort to disguise how frightened he was, nor how happy he was to see her, and that made Martine cry again, and for a while they just rode along like that, holding hands.

After a while Martine felt shy, which she knew was ridiculous under the circumstances, but she let go of his fingers and said, 'What time do you think it is?'

Ben managed a weary smile. 'Why, have you got an appointment?' But he went on quickly, 'We can probably work it out. It was about nine-thirty when the siren went off, and we've probably been in the water for two or three hours. Judging by the position of the moon, I'd say it's between midnight and one in the morning.'

Martine fell silent again and the two of them concentrated on staying awake so they could watch over the others. After a while the numbing cold and the easy rhythm of the dolphins and the endless, rolling ocean, almost flat now that the storm had passed over, had a soporific effect. They began to murmur to themselves about mirages they glimpsed of palm-fringed islands, or steaming bubble baths, or rescue parties bearing mugs of hot chocolate and thick, soft blankets, so that when a lighthouse did actually loom into view – atop a hulking dark outline of land, ragged with palms – they thought it was just another mirage.

The dolphins slowed and stopped. When their passengers didn't respond, they deposited them unceremoniously in the shallows. And even when the seven frozen figures felt solid sand beneath them, even then they couldn't believe it was real, because the rocking motion of the sea had infused their bodies, and they still felt as though they were floating. It was all any of them could do to crawl beyond the fringe of surf, which they did without speaking, the stronger ones helping the others. Then they collapsed on the darkened beach.

Martine's muscles were so sore and wobbly that those final few steps were the most arduous of the night. The air was fragrant and balmy, but the chill had penetrated to the very marrow of her bones and her teeth chattered uncontrollably. When she could go no further, she toppled onto the pillowy sand. Ben dragged her a bit further, beyond the tide's reach, and then he flopped down a few feet away from her. As weak as he was, there was something about his presence which made Martine feel protected. Moments before she lost consciousness, she whispered to him, 'Ben, weren't you afraid of dying?'

'No,' he said quietly. 'I was afraid of not living.'

Martine fell into a sleep which was closer to a coma, with the palm fronds rattling like wind chimes in the breeze and her head full of the dolphins' song.

12

Martine woke to the soothing swish of sea and the sun on her skin. It flowed into her grateful bones like hot honey. She tried opening her eyes but her lashes were crusty with dried salt and at first all she saw was a beach strewn with untidy heaps of clothes and a few life-jackets. Then one of the heaps started snoring. Claudius! Martine couldn't believe it. As if she hadn't been through enough. What had she done in her life to deserve being stuck on a desert island with Claudius?

Further down the beach, Sherilyn was lying on her back, wearing pink pyjamas. Her mouth was open. Her fluffy, polka-dotted dressing gown was gone. On her left was Jake Emery, his lanky, athletic limbs curled into a foetal ball, and on the other side was Lucy Van Heerden, her pale blonde hair splayed over the sand. A large orange crab was making a home in it. Martine debated whether to remove it, but couldn't summon up the energy. Further along the beach lay the sprawled figure of an African boy. Martine's eyes wouldn't cooperate enough for her to be sure, but it looked like Nathan Nyathi. He, too, appeared to be asleep. Her gaze shifted to the last item of clothing and she saw that that was all it was, an item of clothing.

Ben! Where was Ben?

Some of the terror of the previous night returned to rob Martine of what little reserves she had. She scrambled to her feet and stood rocking, her head swimming. The beach felt as unsteady as the deck of a yacht. Gradually the dizziness passed and she took a few steps, wincing at the stiffness in her muscles. Her lips, too, were cracked and swollen. She had a raging thirst. Her jeans and top were still damp on the side where she'd slept on them and her hair was matted with gritty sand. Her stomach growled loudly. She longed for a shower, a coffee, and two or three of Alberto's bacon and fried banana rolls, but those were clearly out of the question. Ben, she had to find Ben.

She began to walk along the beach, and it was only then that her mind unfogged sufficiently for her to take in her surroundings. The sand stretching out before her was of the purest white, though the early morning sunlight gave it a rose glow. It was so clean that it squeaked underfoot as if mice or a litter of puppies were nestling beneath it. Palm trees followed the long, lazy curve of the bay. The turquoise sea was as translucent as bath water. Martine could see a big blue starfish drifting along the bottom of it. In the distance, she could hear the dull crashing of waves, but the water in the bay was tranquil and idyllic, suggesting it was ringed by a coral reef.

But it was the island itself that really got Martine's attention. It didn't look like the sort of island one saw in photographs of Mauritius or the Caribbean. It was a mix of mountainous sand dunes, regular African bush and lush, low-lying greenery, as though the deserts of Arabia had been joined up with Sawubona. A lighthouse was perched on the highest point. There were no obvious signs of human habitation, but the lighthouse was very encouraging. Martine had a dim recollection of coming round briefly at some point during the night and seeing a yellow beam flashing from its tower. If there was a lighthouse with a working light, surely that meant there was a lighthouse keeper?

Martine reached the end of the beach without seeing any sign of Ben. She was staring up at the Everest of rippled chestnut sand, trying to pluck up the courage to return to her fellow castaways and appeal to them to form a search party, when he came tripping over the top of the dune. His black hair was wet and shiny and he was wearing frayed denim shorts, which he'd manufactured somewhat haphazardly from his jeans. Shirtless, he looked slimmer than ever, but his arms were strong and his chest and stomach were ridged with muscle. With his burnt caramel skin, he looked as if he belonged to the island; as if it was his natural home.

'Breakfast,' he called to Martine when he saw her, dipping his chin at the stack of green coconuts he was holding in his arms. He slid the rest of the way down the dune and dropped them at her feet. 'Only one small problem – I haven't been able to find a way to remove their outer husks. They're very tough and fibrous and bashing them against rocks barely makes an impression.'

Martine was so taken aback by the sight of him – particularly since he looked and spoke like a boy on his summer holidays and not like the survivor of a harrowing ordeal – that she was silenced. A concerned frown came over Ben's face and he had to ask her twice if she was okay before she managed to get out, 'I have a knife . . . maybe we can use the knife to cut off the husks?'

Then it was Ben's turn to look astonished as he realized that, not only was she still wearing her pouch, it was a survival kit. He watched wide-eyed as she turned out the contents for him to see, showing him the matches, Swiss Army knife, fishing line, compass and Grace's potions. Everything had stayed clean and dry in the waterproof pouch but the leaves were badly wilted. Their days were numbered.

Ben couldn't believe she had carried them all the way from Cape Town. 'Are they important? We might be able to save them.'

'What are we going to save them with? Coconut milk?'

Ben laughed. He'd cut the husk off the first coconut and now he pierced three little holes in the top of it and handed it to Martine. 'Drink this and I'll show you.'

Martine had never appreciated any liquid more, although it wasn't as coconutty as she was expecting and was really quite sour-tasting and fermented. Still it was wonderfully soothing to her cracked lips and parched throat. When she was done, she broke the brown-bristled shell against a rock. The moist coconut meat inside was sweet and moreish. With every mouthful, she could feel the energy returning to her limbs.

Ben nibbled at his while he worked at de-husking the remaining coconuts. Martine watched, wondering how he'd managed to scrub up so well in the sea. She felt very self-conscious beside him. Her salt-stiffened hair was sticking up like a punk-rocker's Mohawk and she was quite certain she smelled like a day-old haddock. She was very relieved when Ben put the coconuts in the shade and said that he had something to show her. She followed him up the high dune with difficulty, the soft sand sinking like snow beneath her feet, her muscles protesting.

Over the other side, the ground was firmer. Ben led her through palm groves and trees draped with tropical creepers, walking with an enthusiasm she was far from sharing. She plodded behind him, feeling breathless. Her head hurt. Colourful birds skittered through the leaves, but Martine barely noticed them. She was remembering what Alberto had told her about all the snakes on the Mozambican islands.

'Ben, I don't understand why you're so cheerful.' She was unable to keep the frustration out of her voice. 'We nearly died last night, and now we're marooned on an island in the middle of the Indian Ocean. It's a disaster and you're acting like we're on vacation or something.'

'I'm not happy because we nearly died last night, I'm happy because we're alive this morning,' Ben explained. 'I'm happy because the dolphins saved us, which is sort of a miracle, and because we've already found two of the things we're going to need to survive. Obviously, I'd rather be eating breakfast on the *Sea Kestrel,* but whatever happens now it'll be an adventure. A real adventure.'

'You said we've found two of the things we need to survive. We've found food. What's the other thing?'

They'd reached the edge of the trees. Ben stepped aside. Before them, fringed with reeds, was a small lake. 'This,' he said.

'Is that really . . . ?' Martine was reluctant to put what she saw into words in case it, too, turned out to be a mirage.

'Clean water? Well, no, not exactly, but it is fresh water. Just to be on the safe side, use the bandana to strain it into one of the gourds from that monkey apple tree before you drink it, but I'd say it's pretty pure. It's definitely pure enough to bathe in. You'll need to be careful, though. Mozambique has lots of freshwater crocodiles and this kind of habitat is perfect for them.'

Martine, who'd been so eager for a drink and a bath that she'd been poised to leap into the shallows, fully-clothed, decided that cleanliness was not a priority after all. She'd had enough problems with sharks; she didn't need new nightmares about crocodiles. 'Maybe I've had enough of being in water for the time being . . . ' she began.

She stopped. Ben was holding his nose.

'Okay, I take the hint,' she said crossly, 'but if I get attacked by a crocodile, you're going to have to answer to my grandmother.'

As soon as the words were out, it hit her that she'd been so preoccupied with searching for Ben and thinking about how hungry she was and how much her head hurt, she hadn't taken in that there was no guarantee she would see her grandmother or her beloved white giraffe ever again. It was heart-breaking to realize that her grandmother's last memory of her might be of their fight, and that Jemmy would never understand that something had happened to prevent her returning to him. He'd think she'd abandoned him.

Ben saw the anguish on her face and his own sobered. 'Listen, if there's a way off this island, we'll find it, I promise. You *will* see your grandmother and Jemmy again, and I *will* see my mum and dad. But I have a feeling that the dolphins have brought us here for a reason. It's up to us to figure out what that reason might be.'

· 13 ·

Twenty minutes later Martine was drying off in the sunshine at a respectful distance from passing crocodiles and marvelling at how rapidly she'd recovered from the previous night's trauma once she'd had a drink of water and washed the salt and grit from her hair, when there was a blood-curdling screech.

Ben came running out of the trees. He'd climbed up to the lighthouse while she was bathing. 'Do you think one of the girls is in trouble?'

'Oh, I think Lucy probably just found a crab nesting in her hair,' said Martine.

Ben gave her a quizzical look, but didn't ask how she was so sure.

Martine used a gourd to trickle water onto Grace's wilted leaves. She'd found a home for them and the thread of root which bound them together in the fertile soil near the lake. On the one hand there didn't seem much point in trying to revive them, but on the other hand they were symbolic of Grace and Sawubona. It was as if a little piece of both was here on the island with her. That made the scrap of plant as important as her survival kit.

She felt like a new person after her wash and a few gourd's full of water. Her headache had gone. She'd used the knife to cut her jeans into shorts like Ben's, and washed her T-shirt and sweatshirt. They were still a little soggy but the sun was so warm she didn't mind.

As they wandered back to the others, Ben told her about the lighthouse, which was derelict, although solar panels and a timer kept its beam working at night. Alas, there was no friendly lighthouse keeper and no working radio. The only useful thing he'd discovered was a piece of broken sign. It was written in Portuguese but in the centre was a partial word in bold letters, 'BAZ . . . '

'Bazaruto!' breathed Martine. 'I bet you we're on one of the Bazaruto Islands in Mozambique. We were about 100 miles from them at lunchtime yesterday so I guess it's possible. Alberto told me that there are six main islands and some tiny ones, but that they're not all inhabited. Trust us to have landed on an abandoned one.'

At the beach, they collected the coconuts. Ben counted out five.

'Are you really going to give one to Claudius after what he did to you?' Martine asked, unsure whether to be impressed or disgusted.

Ben shrugged. 'It's only a coconut.'

'But you could have drowned without your lifejacket.'

'Yes, but I didn't,' was Ben's reply, and Martine could tell that it was his final word on the subject.

Their fellow castaways were in a huddle on the beach, red-eyed and bedraggled. Lucy was shuddering and inspecting her hair, strand by strand, for wildlife. Sherilyn was so distressed she was practically sitting on Jake's lap. A large orange crab was moving ponderously off towards the sea.

'Well, if it isn't Robinson Crusoe and Girl Friday!' Claudius drawled, but not before Martine caught the flicker of shame or perhaps fear (fear of exposure, she was sure) that passed across his plump gold cheeks. She couldn't look at him directly. It made her too angry. Ben might have been able to forgive and forget, but the sight of a rain-lashed Claudius trying to rip Ben's lifejacket from his body was not something she was going to forget in a hurry.

'Where have you been?' Nathan asked. 'We were starting to worry.'

'Were we?' Jake muttered.

Martine ignored him. 'We've brought you some breakfast,' she said by way of a reply, and she and Ben dished out the coconuts.

Squeals of delight greeted this news. Even Claudius managed a grudging, 'Thanks'. There were sucking noises as they swallowed down the milk, followed by a horrible hawking from Claudius as he spat it out. 'Ugh!' he said, wiping his mouth. 'That's revolting. Where's a soda fountain when you need one?'

He hurled away the coconut and it struck a rock and split open. The remaining milk leaked onto the sand. Grit covered the white meat.

Martine shot a look at Ben, but his face was impassive.

'Claudius, mate, that's not cool,' scolded Jake. 'One of us could have eaten that.'

'Get a grip, Jake,' Claudius said impatiently. 'We'll probably be off this island by dinner time. Provided the *Sea Kestrel* didn't sink—'

'Don't say that!' shrieked Lucy. 'What if Luke has been shipwrecked? What if our friends have all drowned?'

'—which is *highly* unlikely, as the captain would have sent a mayday call for assistance. As soon my father hears I'm missing, he'll launch the biggest air and sea rescue ever undertaken in Southern Africa. We'll be tucking into bacon double cheeseburgers in Maputo in under twenty-four hours. Two days, tops. All we have to do is survive till then.'

His friends looked encouraged, but not entirely convinced.

'What if we're not?' demanded Lucy. 'Have you thought about that? My brother will be going nuts wondering what's happened to me. You should have seen the look on his face when I slid off the edge of the *Sea Kestrel*. If I live to be a hundred I'm never going to forget how the sea looked like boiling black oil from above, but it felt like swimming in a freezer, and how hard it was when I hit it. I thought my back was broken or my head had split open or something.'

There were murmurs from the group as they relived their own nightmarish falls.

'If it weren't for the dolphins, we wouldn't be here right now,' Lucy went on. 'And that's great except that now we're stranded on some desert island in the middle of nowhere. If nobody finds us we'll probably starve to death.'

'It's hard to get lost these days,' Claudius assured her. 'The coastguard has very sophisticated search and rescue equipment.'

'I'm thirsty,' Sherilyn whined.

'So am I,' Nathan sympathized.

'We found fresh water,' Martine told them. 'There's a lake in the valley on the other side of the dunes. Also, Ben went to look at the lighthouse. The bad news is that, although it's a working lighthouse, it runs on solar panels. It's not operated by anyone. The good news is that while he was there, he found a piece of a sign. We think we're on one of the uninhabited islands in the Bazaruto Archipelago.'

'The Bazaruto Archipelago?' Lucy repeated. 'That's a huge tourist destination. Some friends of ours stayed at a luxury lodge on Benguerra Island. That means we're really, really close to civilization. The tourists who visit the islands go deep-sea fishing and cruising and snorkelling all the time. That's fantastic news. That means we'll definitely be rescued.'

'What did I tell you?' said Claudius with a confident grin. 'And since that's the case, I think Crusoe and his friend can find somewhere else to hang out until the rescue boats come. We don't get along with them at school. I don't see why we should have to put up with them on an island as big as this one.'

'But they brought us food,' objected Sherilyn.

'We did say thank you,' Lucy pointed out.

Martine was spitting mad, but she tried to follow Tendai's survival advice about not acting impulsively or making rash decisions. 'Don't you think we should stick together?' she asked, looking to the others for support. 'We're in a survival situation and we should really be helping each other.'

'I'm not being funny,' Lucy said, 'but have the two of you seen a mirror recently? You don't look as if you could cross the street safely by yourselves, let alone help anyone else. Ben doesn't even speak. I agree with Claudius.'

'So do I,' put in Jake.

Nathan and Sherilyn pretended that their mouths were suddenly full of coconut.

'That's settled,' announced Claudius. 'We'll call you when the search party gets here. Until then, stay away from us.'

· 14 ·

As soon as they were out of earshot of the others, Ben said, 'Phew, that's a relief.'

He set down the crab. Much to Sherilyn's horror, he'd scooped it up with his bare hands as they'd left.

'What do we do now?' asked Martine, biting her lip. She was as glad as Ben to be away from the others, but she found it difficult to share his holiday spirit. Tendai had drummed into her that a group of lost kids had more chance if they stayed together, and the first thing this group had done was split.

She was also quite shy. In the two months that Ben had been her unofficial best friend, she'd never actually done any best friend things with him, mainly because she only really saw him at school and he never talked there. Plus, she was not exactly up to speed with best friend etiquette, never having had a best friend before apart from Jemmy.

'I think Claudius and Lucy are right about one thing,' Ben said. 'It's very likely that we'll be rescued, if not by the coastguard then by a tourist boat or some local fishermen. But we can't count on it being a day or two. It might take a couple of weeks, or even a month. We need to survive until then.'

A couple of weeks, or even a month. The reality of their situation hit Martine and a curious thing happened. A calmness came over her. She thought about Grace and the Bushmen paintings on the cave wall, 'Only time and experience will give you the eyes to see them,' the *sangoma* had predicted. Martine had seen them when she was supposed to. That meant that, whether she liked it or not, this was her destiny. This African island, with its fairy-flossed dolphins and squeaking white sand and clear, azure waters. And she owed it to Grace, who had counselled her on her gift, and Tendai, who'd spent hours patiently teaching her the secrets of the African landscape, as well as to Jemmy and even to her grandmother, to return safely to them. She had to wake up, be positive and prepare herself for whatever came next.

She smiled at Ben. 'Should we start by making a shelter?'

His eyes lit up. 'Do you fancy building a fort up at the lighthouse?'

Before leaving the beach, Martine filled her sweatshirt with coconuts and helped Ben search for more crabs. They found five large orange ones and a blue and white one with a shell like a willow-pattern plate. 'Sorry, fellas,' Ben said as he bundled them into his windcheater, pincers waving threateningly.

They didn't have a container so they stopped at the lake and drank as much water as they could. The long climb to the lighthouse meant scaling the high, honey-coloured sand dunes. It was torture. Every stride Martine took created a mini-avalanche, causing her to slip two or three steps back. The sand fell away in sheets. The coconuts seemed to increase in weight as she went. Halfway up, one of the crabs crawled out of a hole in Ben's windcheater, which he had slung across his shoulders in a makeshift rucksack, and crushed his earlobe with its pincers.

'Ow!' he yelled, as his ear turned crimson. 'Ow!' He detached the crab with difficulty and returned it to the windbreaker, telling it that it would be the first to be eaten for dinner if it wasn't careful.

When they did reach the lighthouse, it was worth it just for the view – all Sahara-type dunes, green valleys and white beaches. Seen from above, the turquoise water was streaked with splashes of jade and ultramarine blue. The island itself was triangular in shape. Two sides of it were protected by reef, but the third was pounded by rough seas. Red cliffs reared over a rocky coastline, curving round to a calm bay.

The lighthouse had the year 1902 etched above its

entrance. The tower was more or less intact, but the building attached to it was in ruins and missing most of its roof. The concrete floor was cracked and the steps crumbled beneath their feet. Entire pine trees grew out of yellow fissures in the walls. Red hot pokers nodded in empty doorways. Pine needles whispered in the breeze.

Martine and Ben walked from room to echoing room, establishing which was the most habitable. Every window framed a spectacular vista, although the glass was shattered or gone. A smudge of an island – little more than a sandbar – was just about visible through the midday haze. Martine wondered if it was Death Island. One of Alberto's tales had been about a penal colony on Santa Carolina, centuries earlier. He claimed that at low tide the jailers used to take prisoners to Death Island, a tiny shell sandbar, and tell them that if they could swim the eight kilometres or so back to the mainland – a stretch of water cursed by vicious cross-currents and even more vicious sharks – they'd be exonerated. Needless to say, few did. At high tide the sea completely covered the island, and those who were unable to swim simply drowned.

Martine shuddered at the thought of lives so ruthlessly squandered.

'Ghosts?' Ben asked, and she nodded without saying anything.

They decided to sleep under the stars in the raised living area of what would have been the operating centre of the lighthouse, beside the room with the largest section of roof intact. That way if it rained they could quickly seek shelter. The room would also be useful for storing food during the sweltering days. Ben dragged a couple of rocks across the doorway and set the crabs free to roam around in the shade.

It was when the two of them started to stock their new home that they found they had skills which complemented one another. Martine had learned bushcraft techniques from Tendai and a little bit of islandcraft from Alberto, and Ben had learned how to tie knots and the basics of marine survival from his sailor father. So, for instance, while Martine knew that maintaining body heat in a survival situation was vital, and that one simple way to achieve that was to sleep off the ground, Ben was able to construct the low beds that she envisioned in her head, using a combination of bamboo and palm fronds. He tied them together with reef knots, aided by the strips of bark Martine had collected with her knife.

Of course, none of these things were exactly handy, and they required a further three gruelling trips down the dunes in the heat. While they were gathering bamboo, they discovered that there really were crocodiles. Ben had to do a long-jump-style leap to escape from the jaws of a gargantuan male.

On their last trip up the dunes, they carried four gourds of water, although admittedly they were only half full when they reached their destination. Martine was disappointed that the monkey oranges and cashew nuts Alberto had spoken of were not yet ripe because it was winter. She was absolutely ravenous, and had no idea how they were going to pluck up the courage to cook the innocent scuttling crabs.

While Ben built the beds, Martine tied a bundle of twigs together like the African women did at Sawubona, and swept the floor, choking on the thick dust. Then she gathered kindling and built a fire the way Tendai had taught her, making sure that there was plenty of space between the logs so the fire could 'breathe.' By that time the sun was setting and they climbed up into the old lighthouse tower and had a 360 degree panorama as the ocean turned seven shades of red. There was no sign of the others. Half an hour after the sun slid into the sea, it was dark. Martine, who'd been used to endless summer evenings in England, could never get over the guillotine speed of nightfall in Africa, or the impenetrable blackness of it.

With the 'switching off' of the sun, the temperature plummeted sharply. Night birds and bushbabies began to call and cry out softly from the trees. Martine and Ben picked their way carefully down the lighthouse's steep spiral staircase. In their absence, the fire they'd built had burned down to coals and the warm glow of them lent a homely feel to their living area. They put more wood on it and sat close to toast their arms and legs, which were aching after the assault of the past twenty-four hours.

At length, Ben gave an unhappy sigh and went off to deal with the crabs. His father had taught him how to end their lives humanely, but he was still very reluctant to do it. However, without food their own days would be numbered.

'I thought you were a Buddhist,' said Martine when he

returned. 'Don't Buddhists believe that all living things are sacred, and that nothing should be harmed or injured in any way, not even mosquitoes?'

'Haven't you heard the Buddhist story about the crab?' Ben asked, placing the crabs on the edge of the coals. 'They're pretty crafty. Once upon a time there was this crane living beside a pond packed with fish. Every day he ate until he was stuffed but he found that no matter how many he gobbled, he was never satisfied. He became convinced that if he could somehow eat every single fish in the pond, he'd be truly content. First, though, he had to get them all out of the water. So he told the fish that he knew of another, much more beautiful pond, where he'd be more than willing to carry them. One by one, they believed him, and one by one, they climbed into his beak and were eaten. Eventually, he was so full he could hardly fly but then he noticed he'd left behind a crab. He couldn't bear the thought of such a delicious treat going to waste so he offered the crab a ride to the pond.

'But the crab was smart and told the crane that he knew all about his tricks with the fish and that he had no intention of being devoured. However, he did like the idea of being transported to a special pond. He agreed to go on condition that he could ride on the crane's back, with his pincers around its throat. They were almost at the pond when the crane's greediness got the better of him and he tried to trick the crab into getting down off his back so he could eat him. The crab was so angry that he cut off the crane's head with his pincers, just slicing it off "like a knife through butter!" '

'Charming,' said Martine. 'Maybe I won't have crab for dinner after all.'

Ben grinned. 'That's all right. More for me. Actually Buddhism does allow the eating of meat; we're just not supposed to cause pain. I'm a bit of a mix, though, because I'm also half Zulu and some Zulus believe that fish are from the snake family and that the eating of them is forbidden. But Dad is a sailor and sailors love fish and the sea, so we go fishing together and we eat what we catch. Mostly, though, we do try to eat food that doesn't hurt animals. Buddhists believe that animals are equal to people, although the crabs probably wouldn't take my word for that.'

The night had a winter nip to it and they bent as near as they could to the fire. When the crabs were cooked they used a rock to pound the shells and ate the fleshy white meat with crystals of sea salt they'd found in a dried up rock-pool, followed by more coconut for desert. When the last morsel was gone, they sat in companionable silence and listened to the sounds of the island – the squabbling bushbabies, the whine of the occasional mosquito and the far away hiss of the sea. Behind the windowless frames of the lighthouse, the sky was a curtain of stars.

It wasn't long before Martine's eyelids began to droop with exhaustion. She lay down on the low bamboo frame, rested her head on a pillow made of palm leaves, and fell asleep thinking it the most comfortable bed she'd ever slept on.

15

Over the next two days, Ben and Martine explored every inch of the island – except, of course, the beach where the others were camped out, which they'd named Runway Beach because that was where they'd landed. Martine found it hard to get used to the mix of tropical and African scenery, although there was no denying it was beautiful. There were great, gnarled marula trees alongside coconut palms and hibiscus flowers, and crinkled brick-coloured cliffs towering over rocky beaches or snowy sands over which translucent crabs scampered. And surrounding it all was the sea with its fizzing shades of washed-out blue, like ink dropped on watercolour paper.

At the top of the wind-rippled dunes, they found hundreds of heavy white shells, fossilized and catacombed with minuscule holes. Ben made up a funny story about them being carried there by a prehistoric bird as big as an ostrich. There were also black clay and glass beads which they supposed had been left by the Arab and Portuguese traders, and on the beach itself there were Pansy shells – white, eggshell – delicate creations etched with the petals of a flower. Just around the peninsula, near the end of the cliff, were a stack of rocky shelves, overlooking a picturesque bay. They were not deep enough to be proper caves, but they were secluded and provided welcome shelter in the heat of the day.

The shelves proved a fine lookout point, but the two whole days passed without a single sign of humanity. They did see a couple of planes, but those were commercial aircraft flying so high they were mere specks across the sun, and Martine's tin lid signal would not have been visible to them. From the lighthouse it was possible to see that their classmates had written a huge SOS on Runway Beach, using dark rocks that showed up against the sand, in anticipation of the arrival of Claudius's father. They had also constructed a crude shelter from sticks and palm fronds, although every time the breeze wafted it collapsed. Once they saw someone – it might have been Jake – kicking it in fury.

At night-time the temperature hovered around zero degrees Celsius, but in the afternoons it was scorching hot.

'If this is winter, I don't think I'd like to try Mozambique in summer,' remarked Martine on the third afternoon, fanning her face with a palm frond. She had found a clump of aloes near the lighthouse and was using the gel from the leaves to calm her sunburn.

Ben was fishing on the rocks near the sea's edge, using the line and hook from the survival kit and crab entrails for bait. He had caught two bream, which he'd put in a shaded rock-pool where they could be easily retrieved later, and he was trying for another. But he was distracted. The water-level had dropped with the departing tide and the tip of a wreck had appeared on the edge of the reef. Ben was sure it was a Portuguese galleon. It reared above the crystalline waters.

'I've always wanted to look inside a real wreck,' he said wistfully. 'Imagine the stories it could tell. Imagine the history it's seen. It might even have been a treasure ship. There could be caskets of pearls and gold. Better still, they might contain old journals or maps. It's very unlikely because lots of other people would have investigated it before us, but you never know. We might find something that they missed. Oh, I can't wait to get home and tell my dad about it.'

Martine was fascinated by the wreck herself but she shivered at the thought of tackling the currents again. Bathing on the edge of the lake, or paddling in the clear island shallows, which were as non-threatening as Caracal Junior's swimming pool, was one thing, but never again would she put herself in a situation where there was even a remote chance she might be circled by sharks or fighting to breathe in deep, dark water. The ordeal of the storm was still too fresh in her mind. Her fear of the sea had become a virtual phobia. The wreck was on the edge of the open ocean. Who knew what lurked in the churning depths around it.

'Will you come with me?' Ben asked eagerly. 'I know it's a long way out but we'll be fine if we're together.'

Martine flushed. She wanted so badly to say yes to her friend because she knew how much it would mean to him, but it was impossible. 'I'm sorry,' she said. 'I just can't.'

Ben thought she was probably still traumatised by the storm so he did his best to hide his disappointment. 'That's okay,' he said. 'I understand.'

He went to cast his line again and a movement in the water caught his eye. 'Hey, look! The dolphins are back.'

Martine returned the fishing equipment to her pouch and then she and Ben waded into the bay. At first, the dolphins seemed too busy to notice them. They darted about like quicksilver in pursuit of invisible shoals, so lithe and graceful that it was almost as if upon entering the water they, too, became liquid. On surfacing, they exhaled in soft puffs.

Gradually, their inquisitive nature got the better of them and they swam nearer and nearer. One was bolder than the rest. He separated himself from the pod and sidled up to Martine. There were three V-shaped grooves on his dorsal fin and she recognized him as the dolphin who'd saved her on the night of the storm. He showed off a little, approaching her shyly and then gliding away to turn a few artistic backflips and somersaults. When at last he settled for lying on his side close to Martine, she tickled his chin and the area around his blowhole and pectoral fins. He enjoyed that so much that he rolled belly-up and allowed her to stroke his speckled tummy. His eyes were half-shut in ecstasy. He lolled in the water as if it were as supportive as an armchair.

Ben had seen plenty of dolphins on boat trips with his father, but until the night of the storm he'd never touched one. He, too, had been surprised by the satin-smooth texture of their skin. He also wanted to know how Martine had recognized her dolphin so easily, so she told him what she knew about dolphins' dorsal fins being as unique as giraffes' patches and human fingerprints. That jolted Ben's memory and he recalled that the dolphin who'd carried him had had cookie-cutter-shaped holes in her fins. Shortly afterwards, he spotted her.

'We're not going to hurt you,' Martine told the dolphins. 'You saved us and brought us to this place. We only want to get to know you.'

The dolphins picked up on the gentleness in her voice and her saviour-dolphin's willingness to accept her touch, and their last shred of reserve melted away. They came crowding around with rough trills and whistles.

Their dorsal fins were relatively easy to tell apart, so Ben and Martine decided to name them. Martine called her boisterous dolphin Sun Dancer, because of the way the light glinted on his back as he leapt. Ben christened his dolphin Cookie and another Honey because she had a golden tint in her silver-grey skin. Patch had white splotches on his back – the result of sunburn or battle-scars from a shark attack; Mini was small and elderly – a grandmother dolphin; Rain Queen appeared to be Sun Dancer's wife and Little Storm their baby; and then there were Ash, Steel and Thunder, three bright-eyed boys. They were also named after their colours, but it was their dorsal fins and cheeky faces which provided the real clues to their identity.

Ben had collected a few strands of sea grass and was playing a game of tag with Cookie, so Martine floated in the translucent water, eyes half-shut, and let the sunshine and the presence of the dolphins infuse her being. There were so many exquisite, ingenious and loveable animals on the planet – giraffes for starters – but dolphins, she felt, were different. They were like the chocolate of the animal world. You couldn't get enough of them.

Soon she sensed one of the dolphins approaching. She opened her eyes and saw that it was Little Storm. She stretched out her arms and opened her palms to show him there was nothing harmful in her hands. But the baby dolphin was wary. After each timid advance, he would swim away. He whistled at her a couple of times and Martine tried whistling softly back, experimenting with a song her father had taught her: 'Amazing Grace'. Little Storm mimicked her, and she could have sworn that he'd learned a couple of notes of it. Either way, it seemed to soothe him. He swam up to her and laid his face in her palms, and they floated in the buoyant water looking at one another. For Little Storm, it was a gesture of supreme trust. For Martine, it was unforgettable.

Later, as she and Ben paddled to the shore, Martine said, 'We should name this bay so it can be our special place even after we leave here.'

'Why don't we call it Dolphin Bay?' Ben suggested.

So Dolphin Bay it was.

That evening, Ben cleaned, gutted and filleted the fish from the lake, and Martine picked a few banana leaves in which to wrap them while they cooked, as she'd often seen Tendai do. Unfortunately, the bananas themselves were not yet ripe. They built a new fire and warmed up while they waited for it to burn itself out and turn the wood into coals. Only then did they put the fish on.

Laying her damp survival pouch near the fire to dry, Martine was reminded of her classmates who didn't have matches and faced a third long, cold night, probably without dinner. That made her feel guilty, even though there was no real reason she should since it was she who had attempted to keep everyone together. Earlier that day, while she and Ben were laughing and fooling around with the dolphins, Martine had spotted a couple of figures watching them from the palm trees. When next she'd turned her head, they'd gone. She'd told herself that they could be having fun as well if they'd chosen to, but it was hard not to feel bad.

'I feel guilty, too,' said Ben, guessing her thoughts. 'But I'm trying not to.'

Their supply of firewood was running low, so they left the fish to cook while they went out to find more. They gathered anything combustible they could find and put it into a single pile. For the first time since leaving Sawubona, Martine felt something close to happiness – or at least as happy as it's possible to be when she didn't know when, or if, she'd see Jemmy again.

Her mum and dad would have been proud of how she was adapting, managing, surviving. She hadn't given a thought to being rescued for hours. Being on the island and around dolphins had certainly made her feel differently about things. She was forced to exist in the moment. To take each day as it came. Hopefully some of it would rub off, so that when she did eventually get back to Sawubona, she and her grandmother would work everything out. They would hug and make up. It would all be okay.

When she and Ben had collected enough kindling, they climbed back up to the lighthouse under the blazing white light of a full moon. Far below them, the ocean spilled out like a wizard's cloak, dark blue and speckled with sparkles. The smell of barbecuing fish wafted through the air.

'I wonder what the others are doing?' Martine said, her words muffled by the armful of timber she was carrying. 'I bet you anything *they* haven't managed to catch any fish. I wonder what they're planning to eat tonight?'

Ahead of her, Ben stopped so suddenly that she ran into him. He put down his wood. 'I think we're about to find out,' he said.

Jake and Nathan were sitting in front of the fire in the lighthouse, white flecks of fish dotted around their mouths. Sherilyn's cheeks were so stuffed that she resembled an especially greedy hamster. Lucy and Claudius were reclining on the low bamboo beds. They looked as though they were waiting to be fed grapes.

Jake was the first to spot the aghast faces at the door. 'Hi guys!' he said. 'Thanks for the great dinner. We really appreciate it. Who knew you could cook like that?'

Sherilyn spluttered something unintelligible.

'Even I have to admit that it was pretty good,' Claudius added more coherently. 'Full marks. And this is even better . . . ' He reached under the bed and pulled out the survival kit.

'Leave that alone!' cried Martine. She went to fly at him, but Ben's hand shot out and grabbed her wrist and he held her there, struggling.

'Oooh, temper, temper,' mocked Claudius, and the others laughed. He unzipped the pouch and began pulling out its contents. 'I've been having a rummage through this and it's unbelievably useful. Were you a Brownie in a past life, Martine? Look at this – a knife, matches, fishing line . . . Everything anyone could need on a desert island.

It's almost as if you knew you'd be ending up on one.'

'Give it back to me,' demanded Martine. '*Please.*'

Claudius gave a dramatic sigh, as if the decision were out of his hands. 'Sorry, Martine, no can do. This stuff is very handy.'

Nathan seemed embarrassed but he didn't say anything.

'*Ja,*' said Jake, 'you didn't share with us, so why should we share with you?'

Martine was outraged at the injustice of this accusation. She and Ben had worked like Trojans to create a warm shelter and catch fish for their dinner, and now the others were going to reap the benefits of their labours. It was so unfair. She looked to Ben for support, but none was forthcoming. If anything, he seemed ever so slightly amused.

'You were the ones who didn't want anything to do with us,' she reminded Jake. 'We did want to share stuff with you but you told us to stay away.'

'Yes,' agreed Claudius, 'but you didn't mention that you happened to be carrying a Girl Guide pouch. If you had, we might not have been so hasty.'

Martine was fuming. She lunged at him in a last-ditch attempt to snatch her survival kit, but Ben was too fast for her and he pulled her out of the lighthouse and along the path.

'Let go of me,' said Martine, panting. She wriggled out of his grasp and stood glaring at him. 'Why didn't you *do* something? How could you just let them get away with taking everything from us – our food, our shelter, our survival equipment? What are we meant to do now? Why do you have to be so nice all the time? You're ten times faster and fitter than Claudius. You didn't have to give him your lifejacket on the ship. You could have saved my survival kit if you'd tried. But no, you did nothing. What's worse, you wouldn't let me do anything. Don't you know that sometimes you have to fight for what's right?'

Without a word, Ben began to walk away.

'That's right, just run away,' Martine said scornfully. 'You can't even stand up to a girl. It's true what everyone says about you. You are a wimp. You're pathetic.'

Ben froze in his tracks. He turned around slowly and the lighthouse beam fell on his face. Martine saw the terrible hurt in his eyes.

'What did you want me to do?' he asked quietly. 'Did you want me to hit him? Did you want me to attack Jake or Nathan or even Lucy? Why? Because they were hungry and ate a bit of fish? Because they saw an opportunity for some easy shelter and took it? The sea is full of fish and the island has plenty of shelter. When did fighting ever solve anything?'

Martine didn't answer. She felt as if she was standing outside her body looking down on herself. She knew she was behaving badly but she was powerless to do anything about it.

'I *do* fight,' Ben continued in his soft, steady voice. 'I fight every day to be allowed to be who I am. I just don't do it with my fists, or with words the way other kids do.'

Then he strode away down the dunes and was swallowed by the night.

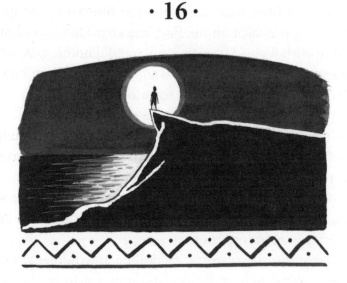

16

It was an odd experience to be utterly alone. Martine felt like a pinprick in a vast, star-speckled universe, standing in a landscape as alien as the mountains of Mars. Every reference point she'd ever had was gone. Her mum and dad were dead. The new life she'd built for herself was an ocean away. Her new family had been torn apart. In a matter of a week, she had fallen out with her classmates; been unkind to her best and only human friend, a boy who had only ever been kind to her; and told her grandmother that she hated her. As a result, the loneliness she had been so scared of at Sawubona had come to find her here, in the loneliest place of all.

Martine felt a lot of emotions but the main one was shame. She wished that Grace was around to envelop her in a mammoth hug and say something wise, or that Jemmy was nearby to nuzzle her and make his musical fluttering sound, but another part of her felt that she didn't deserve a hug or a nuzzle. She listened, hoping to hear Ben's footsteps. But there was only the whisper of waves and the sad whine of the wind, which lifted grains of sand and stung her with them. She wanted to cry, but she knew that crying wouldn't help. People who felt sorry for themselves in survival situations tended not to last very long. She needed to get her head together and prepare for the long night ahead.

After a lingering look at the lighthouse, where the dancing light of the fire set the walls and windows aglow, she set off down the dunes. Her plan was to make her way to the rocky ledges above Dolphin Bay on the far side of the island. There she would be shielded from the worst of the weather and, with any luck, out of the reach of passing snakes or scorpions.

The part of the journey Martine found most unnerving was the walk through the copse of trees near the lake, where blustery sea winds threw leaping-panther shadows. She was too heart sore to be truly afraid, but she was definitely relieved when her toes sank into the squeaking sand of Runway Beach. It took another fifteen minutes to reach Dolphin Bay, and her muscles were quivering with tiredness by the time she climbed the slick rocks of the cliff. She was starving, too – not that she could have eaten a thing.

The ledge she chose smelled of bird's nests and fish bones, but it was dry and sheltered. Martine sat on the edge of it and gazed out at the moon and the glittering sea beneath it. There was some comfort in knowing that the same moon would be shining on the white giraffe and the other animals at Sawubona. And, of course, on her grandmother, who would probably be finishing dinner around now.

But Martine's other life, life at Sawubona, seemed a million miles away. She tried to remember how things were before they got so mixed up – before she upset everyone she cared about. That got her thinking about how small and petty the causes of arguments were. Mostly they came down to one person believing that they were more right than somebody else, or another person wanting what someone else had.

That's what had happened tonight.

She lay down on the rock but the hard, chilly stone made sleep impossible. She sat up again and that's when she heard it – a cough. It came from the next ledge, she was sure of it. Ben! Immediately Martine felt better. Even though they weren't speaking – even though Ben probably thought her the most monstrous girl he knew, it was good to have him near by. She wondered if he was as cold as she was and was jolted by an awful thought. Ben had no warm clothing with him. When they'd been gathering wood, he'd been bare-chested and in shorts, because she'd teased him about the goosebumps all over his body. And after the row at the lighthouse, he'd been so concerned about preventing her from getting into a fight that he hadn't thought to grab his T-shirt and windcheater as he went. Martine knew that if she was freezing in a T-shirt and sweatshirt, Ben would be feeling even worse.

For half an hour, she plotted and schemed about hiking all the way back to the lighthouse and snatching her survival kit or, failing that, a red hot ember which she could use to start a fire. Then she remembered something. During one of her attacks of guilt over their fellow castaways, she'd taken a couple of matches from the pouch with the intention of giving them to anyone except Claudius if the opportunity arose. But it never had.

She dug in her pocket. They were still there.

Minutes later, Martine was foraging along the shoreline in pitch darkness in a bid to find dried palm fronds, coconut husk, pieces of driftwood or anything else that might burn. It was horrible rummaging around blindly, not knowing whether a scorpion was about to sting her or a vengeful crab was waiting to crush her fingers with its pincers – she kept thinking of the crab in the Buddhist story, slicing off the crane's head 'like a knife through butter', but she persevered until she had two big piles of wood. Then, using her sweatshirt, she transported them back to the ledges.

Ben was curled up on the edge of the fluttering moonlight, bare shoulders against the bare rock. He was asleep. Goosebumps covered his body and his lips looked blue. As quietly as possible, Martine stacked the logs the way Tendai had shown her and lit the kindling. The flames crackled into life. Ben never stirred, but as the driftwood began to smoulder and the heat spread his skin regained its smoothness and he stopped shivering. Martine made one more trip down the rocks for extra wood, which she stacked close by. Only when she was satisfied that the fire would burn for most of the night did she return to her own ledge. She built herself a smaller version of Ben's fire and lay down beside it, tired to the bone. Not even the unforgiving rock could keep her from sleep.

It rained all morning. Martine sat under the overhang, watching the still, empty sea. Alberto had told her that in his youth it had never rained in the winter, but that this year there had been floods. She neither heard nor saw Ben. Around midday, she couldn't stand the suspense any longer and poked her head around the rocks. He was gone, although he had taken care to sweep the ash, coals and unburned bits of wood into a pile so that when he returned the embers beneath would be hot enough to restart the fire. Martine took that as an indication that he'd appreciated her efforts, but not that he'd forgiven her.

At lunchtime the rain stopped and the sky turned a milky blue. The birds celebrated with a burst of song. For a multitude of reasons, Martine did not want to encounter the lighthouse thieves, so she stayed in her shelter until hunger drove her out. Even then, she merely dashed to the nearest coconut palm for a couple of coconuts and dashed back. Removing the husks without the knife was a trial. Martine spent nearly an hour using a sharp rock to liberate the white flakes inside. But all she got for her trouble was a stomach ache. It didn't fill her up. She ventured down again to the rock pools and scooped up a tangled pile of slimy seaweed. After several failed attempts to cook it on the fire, she ate it as it was. It was salty, rubbery and completely vile, but it cleared her head and made her feel less tearful.

Mid-afternoon, the dolphins appeared in the bay and she decided to go down and talk to them. They would cheer her up. They would make her believe that absolutely everything was going to be all right. That Ben would be her friend again. That Gwyn Thomas wouldn't always be annoyed with her and wouldn't send her away from Sawubona. That she would see Jemmy again.

She was standing in the frothy fringes, adjusting to the water temperature, when she noticed that the departing tide had uncovered the wreck and it reared once more from the sea which had conquered it. It seemed to beckon to her. Miss Volkner had told the class that no less than eleven Portuguese galleons had been dashed to pieces on the rocks along South Africa's Transkei coast between the mid-16th and 17th centuries, and that many were thought to be treasure galleons. Ben had thought that this wreck might be one too, but now she would never know. She had turned down the chance to go out to it with him, and investigating the old galleon without him would be both pointless and insane. That was the thing about having a friend. You could do things that weren't really possible on your own. Friends made you brave. Friends made things fun.

Of course, fun was going to be in short supply from now on.

Unless . . . Martine swallowed hard. Unless she did something to win back Ben's trust. Something like . . . But no, it didn't bear thinking about. Venturing out alone to the reef, where the only thing holding back the full ferocity of the Indian Ocean was a fragile wall of coral, was not a risk worth taking. There was no telling what treacherous currents swirled around its edges, or what sea monsters lurked in the rusty carcass of the wreck.

But the thought wouldn't go away. Ben had been so incredibly excited at the prospect of finding a casket containing old journals, maps or bits of treasure. 'It's very unlikely,' he'd said, 'but you never know. We might find something they've missed.' Perhaps *she* could find something. Then she could present Ben with a ship's compass or a gold coin as evidence that his friendship was so important to her that she'd been prepared to overcome her worst fears to get it for him. Surely that would be enough to restore his faith in her?

But at the back of her mind two things kept nagging at her. What if she got into trouble in the water and nobody knew where she was? Worse still, what if the rescue boats came and nobody could find her, and they thought she was dead or lost at sea, and they went without her and she was left alone on the island forever? What then?

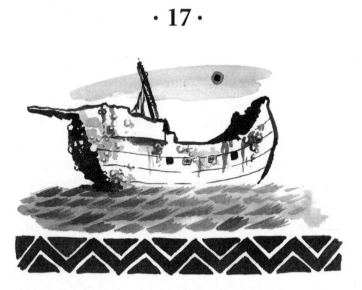

17

The first sign that swimming out to the wreck might not be the best idea she'd ever had came when the dolphins kept blocking her path to it. They lay on their sides and squeaked and looked impossibly cute. They turned their bellies to the late afternoon sky and did dolphin backstroke. They did rolls and acrobatics and half a dozen other tricks.

Initially Martine interpreted it all as a game, but when the end result of everything they did was to prevent her from swimming in the direction of the reef, she became convinced the dolphins were trying to tell her that there was something dangerous there. Either that or they had become drunk on rain water, as the Tsonga believed they sometimes did.

'What are you trying to tell me, Sun Dancer?' she asked. 'What's wrong, Patch and Honey? Is there something bad out there? Are there sharks out there?'

Before wading out to the dolphins, Martine had made a trip to the lake to fetch a couple of reeds. In times gone by, warriors and hunters had used reeds as makeshift snorkels in order to cross rivers or approach enemies or animals undetected, and she was going to attempt to do the same while searching for treasure. She'd broken the reeds into pieces of varying lengths. After a brief experiment in the shallows, she'd chosen a medium-length one. Periodically, she scanned the beach for Ben in the hope that he'd come rushing over to stop her and to tell her that what had happened the previous night was a silly misunderstanding, and that *of course* he'd be her friend again. But the beach stayed empty.

While she'd been at the lake, a stiff breeze had picked up and now she watched as a wave from the open sea dashed against the reef, sending an avalanche of spray across the wreck. Martine's nerves combined unhappily with the stew of seaweed and coconut in her stomach. One false move and she'd be swept into the ocean.

She started to swim for the galleon, but again Sun Dancer blocked her way. The other dolphins crowded round her and, sad and frightened as she was, she couldn't help smiling. They had a way of looking at her that was very wise but also very childlike and cheeky. She suddenly realized that, far from being isolated, she was surrounded by animals, and that they would always accept her the way she was. That, even if every human being she knew gave up on her, or was angry with her, she would still have her gift.

It was a heartening thought and it gave her the courage she needed to kiss Sun Dancer goodbye, push him gently but firmly aside, and swim for the reef. Nevertheless, she found it disturbing that the dolphins refused to accompany her. It was almost as if there was an invisible line in the bay that they knew not to cross. Martine herself crossed that imaginary line with trepidation.

The wreck was much further than it had seemed from the beach, and Martine had to cling to its rusting side and rest for several minutes when she finally reached it. When she saw how close she was to the tumultuous waters of the Indian Ocean, her fear returned. At intervals, spray splattered the wreck and a powerful current tugged at her limbs. The insanity of her mission came home to her. Surely there were easier ways to win back Ben's friendship?

Still it seemed a shame to turn back, so she tested the reed again to be on the safe side. It was quite effective. It would have been nice to have a mask, but the water was so clean and the fish so brilliantly coloured it didn't matter.

As far as she could tell, the galleon had run aground on the reef and sunk right where it was. Martine wondered what had become of its crew. She understood all too well the terror they must have felt as white water plumed from the bottom of the boat. There would have been mayhem on board as men, doubtless the worse for wear on rum and without lifejackets, were swamped by the in-rushing sea. Had their caskets of pearls and gold – if indeed that's what they were carrying – gone down with them? Had they made it to shore? Had they ever been rescued? Or had their skulls become homes for fish and, over time, become one with the brain-like coral?

These macabre thoughts were pushed from her head by the otherworldly beauty of the reef. There were blue starfish and red and white ones; fat-lipped parrot fish in glorious shades of mauve, pink and purple; angel fish with yellow and black stripes; and a sprawling octopus which looked like a jellified cartoon ghost. Best of all, there were half a dozen turtles. They were a deep-brown with patterned cream grooves and they sailed lazily through their undersea world with their stumpy legs waving. It seemed impossible that such cumbersome creatures should float, but float they did, their prehistoric heads comically surveying their surroundings.

Slowing every now and then to suck in oxygen through her reed – which was easy enough so long as it remained perfectly upright, but punished her with mouthfuls of salty water when it didn't – Martine glided through the rainbow aquarium. She was surprised to find she was enjoying herself.

At a certain point, shafts of gilded light illuminated the jade depths and she guessed that the sun would soon be setting. She was about to give up her quest and return to the surface when a metallic glint caught her eye. She took a big gulp of air from the reed and dived down to it. As she neared it she saw that it wasn't the sunken treasure it had appeared to be from a distance, but a link in a thick cable. There was nothing old-fashioned about the cable. It was very modern and appeared to be very new.

Martine knew she should be getting back to the beach, but was reluctant to leave without investigating further. A cable suggested communications or electricity and there was always the possibility that it might be connected to something that could lead to them getting off the island. That would impress Ben as much as any treasure would have done. She returned to the surface for more air and swam down again. As she drew nearer to the cable, she spotted another metal band, then another and another. There wasn't just one cable; there was a whole grid of them! A virtual latticework of clear plastic tubing was snaking its way under the sea, tapering into the blue distance.

Martine was about to give one of the cables a tug when a manta ray came flapping towards her. Its black, diamond-shaped wings billowed out like a highwayman's cape. Martine knew that manta rays rarely harmed humans but its size was intimidating and she moved to one side so as not to be in its path. It changed direction and headed straight for her. She shifted again, but it kept coming. The closer it got, the less friendly it looked and the more it resembled a Stealth bomber jet she'd seen on the news in England. Its wings filled her whole vision.

Then it cannoned into her like a charging bull.

'Bl-bl-uhggh,' spluttered Martine as she was propelled to the surface, gagging on seawater. 'Bubblug-h-uhh . . . '

An instant later, there was a muffled, undersea explosion. The force of the blast had a water-cannon effect, flinging Martine upwards and outwards; but the ray caught the full impact. Bits of cartilage, tissue and manta ray skin rained down on the sea like lava.

Martine screamed.

Ben burst from the water beside her, frightening her almost as much as the explosion had done, 'Martine! Martine, speak to me. Are you okay? Where are you hurt? Here, hold on to me.'

Martine was in shock. She couldn't believe that a living creature had been blown apart right before her eyes. She couldn't stop shaking. Her ribs, where the manta ray had barrelled into them, felt as if they'd been through a crusher. 'B-Ben,' she finally got out, 'w-what are you doing here?'

'I saw you swimming out to the wreck and I followed because I was worried about you. But never mind about that now. Did you see what caused the explosion? Was the wreck booby-trapped? Did you touch something?'

'No. I mean, I don't know. I found these cables on the sea-bed and I was on my way to take a closer look at them when this manta ray knocked me sideways. It sort of came after me. Then there was just a bang and a blur of red and white. Oh, Ben, the poor ray. What happened? Was it a bomb?'

Ben was treading water, taking as much of Martine's weight as he could. Blood trickled from a gash on her upper arm, mushrooming into the water and then dissolving into nothing. Above the horizon, a washed-out sunset indicated that they had perhaps half an hour before the African night descended. 'It sounded like an underground mine of some kind,' he said darkly. 'We need to get you back to the beach fast. Do you think you can swim?'

A sudden, unnatural wave rippled across the surface of the sea inside the reef, which had become glassy again as if the blast had never happened.

'What was that?' panicked Martine, clutching at Ben's arm, and then they heard it, the snap of sails and the slap of a boat hull against water. A dhow appeared from around the other side of the island, bounding over the rolling waves.

'A rescue boat,' cried Martine. She raised an arm painfully and opened her mouth to shout.

'No!' Ben warned. 'Those might be the men who laid the mine. Dive deep *now*!'

The wind was strong and the dhow was approaching the mouth of the reef at speed. Martine had time for only one gulp of air before Ben pulled her beneath the surface. Seconds later, the sea boiled white and the dhow's rudder flashed over their heads. Had they moved any slower it would have smashed into them.

Ben swam strongly for the wreck, Martine behind him. The fading of the sun meant that the hulk of the galleon was barely visible underwater. It seemed a long way in the greeny dark. Martine had lost her reed in the blast and her lungs were on fire by the time she felt the ship's grainy side beneath her fingers. She and Ben surfaced cautiously and gasped for breath as quietly as they could.

The dhow had anchored and its sails were down. There were four Africans on board. Two were clad in shirts and trousers; the others were in wetsuits.

By now, a gloomy twilight shrouded the bay, and one of the divers produced a spotlight. He held it up with his right hand and pointed at the sea – which was gory with the remains of the ray – with his left. He said something in a dialect Martine didn't understand.

Ben strained his ears. 'He's saying that something big has died,' he translated. 'Probably a shark or a ray, but not a human being.'

The taller of the two men in shirt and trousers barked aggressively at the diver. He seemed to be questioning this verdict. The diver handed him the spotlight and picked up a spear-gun, and then he and the second diver flipped backwards off the boat. They entered the water with barely a splash. Ben and Martine looked at each other in trepidation. If the divers checked the wreck, they'd be discovered.

'Quick,' whispered Ben, 'up here.'

He clambered onto a ledge about as big as a shoebox and pulled Martine up beside him. They clung to each other for balance. Blood seeped from the graze on Martine's arm, trickling down her bicep. Salt had penetrated the wound and she winced at the sting of it.

The divers appeared in the water below them, the torches on their helmets lighting up the nooks and crannies of the galleon. A tickle came into Martine's throat. Her face turned red and her eyes began to water. The divers separated. One swam out through a hole in the ship's side to check the reef; the other swam directly beneath them. The tickle in Martine's throat was excruciating. Her whole face contorted with the unbearable itch of it. Finally it erupted in a combination cough-sneeze. The sound ricocheted around the wreck.

The diver's head popped out of the water. He had a spear-gun in his hands, cocked and ready to fire. He shouted through the echoing hull to the men on the dhow, apparently asking if they had heard anything.

Their reply was accompanied by laughter. From the sounds of things, they were making jibes about him hearing the voices of long-dead sailors.

The diver scowled. He was so close they could have bent down and touched him, but he was preoccupied with examining the underbelly of the wreck and it never occurred to him to look up. Satisfied that there was nothing more hostile there than a shoal of striped fish and a single bemused turtle, he tucked the spear-gun in his belt and sank beneath the water. There was a snap of cloth as the dhow's sails billowed. A minute later, Martine and Ben were alone with the wind and sea.

They swam back to the shore in darkness. All the way there, Martine kept thinking about what might have happened if Ben hadn't shown up. She could have panicked after the explosion and tried to get back to the beach before she was ready, got cramp and sunk to the bottom of the sea. She could have been kidnapped, or even shot with a spear-gun. She tried to thank Ben and to apologize for hurting him but he hushed her, telling her to save her energy for the swim. Halfway across the bay, the dolphins came fussing round. Martine hung gratefully on to Sun Dancer's dorsal fin and was given a ride in.

As she clambered tiredly up the cliff, it occurred to her that she need never be afraid of deep water again, because what, in the ordinary course of events, could possibly be worse than falling into a stormy sea from a great height, half-drowning in tsunami-sized waves, being circled by sharks, battered by a manta ray, and almost being blown to bits by an undersea mine? After this, the swimming pool at Caracal Junior would feel as safe as a bathtub.

Half an hour later, they were sitting by a fire on Ben's rock ledge, drying a slimy, unappetising heap of seaweed for dinner. It hissed and spat while Ben cleaned the graze on Martine's arm with fresh water he'd fetched earlier that day from the lake, binding it loosely with his red bandana. They were both deep in thought. The same thing was going through both their minds: What should we tell the others?

Should we tell the others?

Martine broke the silence. 'The ray saved my life,' she said suddenly. 'Somehow he knew what was going to happen. So did the dolphins. They tried to stop me.'

'What kind of people would plant an undersea mine in an area with so much marine life?' Ben said, with uncharacteristic anger. 'The ray must have swum into some sort of trip wire and detonated it. Somebody or some organisation has gone to a lot of trouble to make sure that something underwater stays untouched or undiscovered. The dhow was on the scene within minutes of the explosion. That means it was probably anchored, or sailing nearby. But what was the mine protecting? The cables or the wreck? Maybe there is buried treasure there after all.'

They were eating shrivelled kelp and pulling faces at the foul saltiness of it when a figure appeared at the far end of the beach. It was moving swiftly through the darkness, as if the person was running at tremendous speed.

Ben sighed. 'What now?'

Martine rolled her eyes. Whatever it was, it couldn't be good. As the figure neared the foot of the cliff, they saw it was Lucy. Her hair was flying in the sea wind. She scaled the slippery rocks and pulled herself weakly up onto the ledge. When she stepped into the firelight, Martine saw that she was a wreck. She bore no resemblance to the well-groomed, tennis-club girl she'd been on the ship. Her hair hung in rats' tails, her white tracksuit was filthy, and her eyes were spidery squiggles of red.

'It's Claudius,' Lucy said in a small voice. 'There's been an accident. We need your help.'

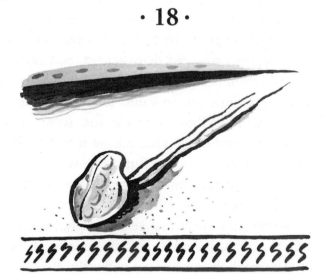

18

Claudius lay unconscious on the sand, so colourless and lifeless in the glow of the torch that if it weren't for the red weals on his belly, he would have blended into it. His face, lips and neck were swollen. His breathing was shallow and laboured. A short distance away from him was the Portuguese man-o'-war responsible for his condition, its top a clear, gas-filled bubble, its tentacles trailing like purple-blue spaghetti almost the width of the beach. It looked too pretty to be dangerous.

Jake was pacing up and down, periodically squatting beside his comatose friend, saying, 'Claudius, mate, you stay with us, you hear?'

Sherilyn was even more of a mess than Lucy. She was sitting on the sand in her crumpled pink pyjamas, wringing her hands. 'We're going to die here,' she said plaintively. 'I'll never see my mum and dad again. This island is going to kill us and all they'll find is our bones.'

The only person doing anything constructive was Nathan, who was going back and forth to the ocean's edge like an automaton, filling a gourd with seawater and trickling it over the weals on Claudius's stomach in an attempt to soothe the inflammation. Martine remembered her dad telling her that vinegar or urine were the best treatments for jellyfish stings, but the man-o'-war was a different species and had a reputation as one of the most venomous creatures in the sea.

'We thought because your dad was a doctor, you might know some first aid or something,' Lucy said in the same small voice to Martine. 'We've tried everything.' Shamefaced, she handed over the survival kit. 'We even tried pouring some of the stuff you had in bottles over the red patches but nothing worked.'

Martine could have wept. Grace's lovingly made potions had been wasted in the sand. The fishing hook and line was missing. Other items were covered in grit. She zipped it up so she didn't have to look at it, and knelt beside Claudius. As they'd run over, she'd felt many conflicting emotions about her tormentor, few of them good. She'd been quite sure that he was being a hypochondriac; that they'd get all the way across the island to find him faking some medical drama just so he could be the centre of attention. But those feelings and doubts left her as soon as she saw him. It was obvious he was critically ill. He was straining so hard to breathe that the veins were practically popping from his neck and his pulse was so weak that Martine had difficulty finding it.

She tilted his head back to ensure his airways were clear, and stood up. 'There's nothing I can do,' she said. 'There's nothing any of us can do. He's had a severe allergic reaction to the sting. I think he's gone into anaphylactic shock. Unless he gets to a hospital fast, he'll probably die.'

Lucy went almost as pale as Claudius, Nathan threw his gourd into the sea and Jake swore softly. Sherilyn burst into tears again.

Ben said, '*You* can help him.'

Five mouths dropped open – Martine's, because she was so stunned to hear Ben break his silence in front of their classmates, and the others, because in the entire three and a half years they'd known him, he'd never uttered a syllable.

'What did you say?' Lucy said incredulously.

'I knew it!' Jake cried. 'I *knew* you could talk. I knew it was an act.'

'Shut up, Jake,' snapped Lucy. 'Claudius is about to die and all you can think about is yourself. Ben, what do you mean about Martine helping him? Martine, if you know a way to save him, do it. I know he's given you a lot of grief. We all have. I'm sorry about the lighthouse and I feel really bad about your survival kit. But can't you forget about that for now? If you help Claudius we'll make it up to you, I promise. '

'It's not that,' Martine told her. 'None of that matters now. Claudius needs treatment only a hospital can give him. He needs allergy medication or some antidote to the man-o'-war venom, and if his heart stops he's going to need to be resuscitated to get it going again.'

'What about that black magic thing you do?' Jake demanded. 'What about that thing you did with the goose at the Botanical Gardens in Kirstenbosch?'

Martine looked at him. She'd once healed an Egyptian goose with a broken wing during a school visit to the botanical gardens in Cape Town, but it was not a happy memory. The part with the goose was, but afterwards the group of kids who'd witnessed the healing – of whom Jake was one – had chased her with sticks, chanting, 'Witch! Witch! Witch!'

She snapped back to the present. 'I don't do black magic,' she told Jake. 'It's the opposite of black magic. Sometimes I help animals a little, that's all. I can't help people.'

'Yes, you can,' Ben repeated. 'You *can* help him.'

There was such conviction in the way he said it that Martine, conscious of what Ben had done for her that afternoon, knelt down beside Claudius without another word and laid her hands on him. Almost immediately her palms began to heat up, just as they had done with the goose and the dolphin, and she could feel a powerful energy flowing through her. But there was a problem. The energy went as far as Claudius's skin and then stopped as if blocked by an impenetrable barrier. Martine concentrated harder, but there was no improvement in Claudius's condition. If anything, he grew even paler and his breathing became more ragged. That's when she knew for certain that her healing gift was for animals and not for people.

So she thought about Grace instead and the wisdom of the grandmothers through the ages, trying to fathom what they would do if they were her. She remembered the night that Grace had come to her in the Memory Room in the caves at Sawubona and had given her a crash course in traditional medicine. Was there anything she had learned then that would help? Grace had spoken a lot about toxins and venoms, but there seemed to be hundreds of variations – poisons that attacked nerves or cells, or clotted blood, or shut down the immune system. It took years of *sangoma* study to get to grips with the antidotes. Martine had a couple of hours at most to find one for Claudius. Meanwhile, his hands, feet and face were swelling to elephantine proportions.

Grace had told her on the day she stopped the bus that when the time came she would know what to do, but Martine didn't. She didn't have the faintest idea.

She concentrated harder. Soon she began to feel light-headed and peculiar. The scene at the beach swam away and she saw smoke and Africans in animal masks and then, out of nowhere, a mental picture of Grace's plant sitting in the blue mineral water bottle in her cabin on *Sea Kestrel* came into her head.

The beach scene, with its deathly-still patient and circle of frightened faces, came rushing back to Martine. 'Is there another name for a man-o'-war?' she asked.

They stared at her blankly.

'Oh, please think. Does it have another name? Do they call it anything else?'

'Umm, uh, a bluebottle,' Jake answered. 'Some people call it a bluebottle.'

'The leaves,' she said to Ben. 'We need Grace's leaves.'

He was gone before she had finished the sentence.

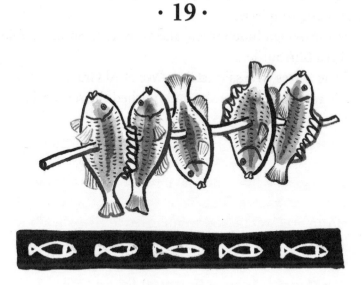

19

M artine sat with her knees scrunched up, watching Claudius's chest rise and fall. For months, she'd thought him one of the most arrogant, unpleasant boys she ever had the misfortune of meeting. Now, as day broke muted and grey across a motionless sea, all she could think was how good it would make her feel if he woke up.

Little by little, Martine realized, the island was changing them. The evening before, Lucy, who'd never previously exhibited the slightest interest in anything other than fashion accessories, shopping and herself, had worked as hard as the boys to construct a shelter to protect Claudius from the elements, and then she had insisted on taking the first shift to watch over him, sitting up all night long before waking Martine shortly before dawn. Now she was asleep, spread-eagled on the sand, snoring faintly.

Even Sherilyn had pulled herself together enough to help gather firewood in the creepy-crawly-haunted darkness. But the biggest change was in Nathan, who was a city boy through and through and had always gone out of his way to avoid contact with wild beasts and the outdoors. At school, he was obsessively neat and had never been known to have a wrinkle or stain on his uniform. And yet he had volunteered to rise when it was still dark and go with Ben to try to catch fish without a hook or line. An embarrassed Jake had confessed to losing Martine's fishing equipment the first time he used it. He and his friends had eaten nothing but coconut for days. So Ben and Nathan were going to try an old islanders' trick to get some.

One of the Mozambican sailors on the ship had told Ben that, in the absence of line, island fishermen would sometimes crush the leaves of the lulla palm, spoon the juicy mixture into a rock pool and wait for the fish to become intoxicated. Meanwhile, they would block the fishes' exit to deeper water. When the fish were rolling drunk, the men would simply scoop them into a net, using sand to protect their hands from the spiky gills.

Since they weren't sure which, if any, of the species of palms that grew in groves on the island were lulla palms, the boys were going to take sample fronds from each and hope that the lulla was among them.

'We don't have a net,' Ben said, with a sly sideways glance at his assistant, 'but Nathan has already offered to give up his shirt!'

Nathan's squawks of protest could be heard halfway down the beach. Martine waved them off and returned to her unconscious patient. It had been a traumatic night. Ben had taken over an hour to find Grace's plant, because he'd been up at the lighthouse when she'd planted it at the lake, and he'd had great difficulty locating it by torchlight. By the time he reappeared with the leaves, Martine had got cold feet about squeezing their milky sap directly onto the weals on Claudius's stomach and legs. Then again, doing nothing could be disastrous. It was Nathan who eventually convinced her to take a chance on the leaves by suggesting the group make a pact. They would each put a hand on Martine while she was administering the sap so they all shared responsibility for the outcome. So that's what they did.

To begin with, the outcome had been as bad as it could possibly be. The weals on Claudius's skin had turned a horrendous colour in the firelight, and he had writhed and moaned in his unconscious state. Martine was quite sure she'd killed him. But after ten minutes or so the high colour faded and the weals had slowly begun to shrink. Over the next couple of hours, the swelling around his neck and face went down and his breathing became more regular. But he had remained unconscious throughout the night.

Now Martine was alone with him. Lucy and Sherilyn

had managed to sleep through Ben and Nathan's fishing preparations, and Jake, who was restless, had gone to the lighthouse to bring down anything that looked as though it might be useful until they could move Claudius. They were all trying to put a brave face on, but an air of desperation had hung over the group the previous evening. Nobody wanted to say out loud that they had been on the island for coming up to five days and they had not seen so much as a glimmer of a search party, tourist or fisherman. And with Claudius at death's door, Martine and Ben had decided that it wasn't a good time to mention undersea mines and spear-gun carrying divers at the wreck.

Martine wondered what was going to become of them. They were all so certain they were going to be rescued. But what if they weren't? What if the men on the dhow came ashore first? What if Claudius never came out of his coma?

It seemed to her that there were a lot of 'what ifs' on the island, and none of them were pleasant.

All at once Claudius's eyes flew open as if he'd been startled awake. He stared around in bewilderment. 'Mum!' he blurted out. 'Mum!'

'Claudius, it's me, Martine. You're still on the island.'

Claudius took in the reed shelter and the white sand and palm trees visible through the entrance and took a ragged breath. In a strange, raspy voice, he mumbled almost to himself, 'It looked so pretty in the water. I was swimming and I tried to catch it. It was like touching fire, only I couldn't get away from it. I was all tangled up in it. I felt as if I was being burnt alive. I was screaming at Jake because he was too scared to take it off me, and then I couldn't feel my legs any more.'

'It's okay,' Martine said, shaken. 'It's okay. You've had an allergic reaction to a Portuguese man-o'-war sting, but you're safe now. You're going to be all right.'

She tried a smile, and even that was an odd sensation because Claudius was not someone she'd ever imagined smiling at. 'Would you like some water?'

He nodded and she held a gourd to his lips and, with some difficulty, supported him as he drank. He lay back down again, facing the wall of the shelter, and was quiet for a long time. Martine thought he'd gone back to sleep and she dozed a little herself. She was awoken by a hoarse, 'Why?'

'Why what?' Martine asked sleepily, although she already knew what he meant.

Claudius rolled over. His cheeks were sunken and his skin tinged with yellow. 'Why did you do it? Why did you help me after the things I've done to you and Ben?'

There was no easy answer, so Martine just said, 'You were very ill. Anyway, it wasn't really me who helped you. It was Grace. She's a traditional healer. She gave me the plant which cured you.'

'Well, she shouldn't have!' Claudius burst out, his voice strained and unsteady. '*You* shouldn't have. I don't deserve to be cured. I wish the dolphins had never saved me. I wish I was dead. You saw what I did to Ben on the ship. I'm a coward.'

Martine had spent a lot of hours thinking much the

same thing, but when Claudius said it himself, she saw that Ben was right. He deserved pity not contempt.

She shook her head. 'We've already forgotten about that.'

It was a lie, but if ever a lie could be justified it was now. 'Everybody does silly things when they're frightened,' she consoled him. 'Anyway, you're not a coward. You were the least scared person on the *Sea Kestrel* at the start of the storm. I heard you telling Luke you were going to stay below deck and watch a film while everyone else was panicking up above. And you helped your father sail your yacht through a hurricane in the Cayman Islands. That takes real guts.'

Claudius said brokenly, 'It isn't true about the yacht, you know.'

'What isn't true? You mean you don't really have a yacht?'

'*Ja*, we have a yacht. And not just any yacht, we have a yacht which once belonged to one of the richest men in Greece. No, I mean it's not true about the hurricane, or about my father asking me to take the wheel. My dad doesn't know one end of a yacht from another, and even if he did, I'm the last person he would trust with it. I did see a hurricane when I was in the Cayman Islands, but it was on the news in our hotel room. Our windows were lashed by wind and rain and the palm trees were bending double, but we were never in any danger. The eye of the hurricane never came within fifty miles of us. A father and son came on the television and talked about how they'd battled the storm in their little boat, and the

156

father was so proud of his son's heroism I decided to pretend that their story was mine.'

He looked away. 'I spend a lot of time watching TV in hotel rooms when my mum and dad are out at cocktail parties with their rich and famous friends. Those kinds of people don't like kids around, especially fat ones.'

Martine pictured her own life at Sawubona – the campfire breakfasts with Tendai where he would talk to her about bushcraft and Zulu legends; the newly-cut-grass scent of Jemmy and the feel of his whiskers when he nuzzled her; the homely evenings with her grandmother when they'd celebrate the successful rehabilitation of a sanctuary orphan with a special African dinner. She realized then how fortunate she was. Yes, she'd lost her parents, but they'd given her more love than many people had from families who were with them for a lifetime. And her grandmother constantly showed Martine that she cared with actions, even if she couldn't always do it with words.

'Is that why . . . why you're not very nice to us?' she asked Claudius. 'Because you're unhappy?'

'Is that why I bully you, you mean? You can say it. No, I give you a hard time because you're the opposite of me; because I envy you. Because your life seems so simple, and because you don't seem to want, or need, anything apart from your white giraffe and your friends at Sawubona. Because even though Ben doesn't speak, it's obvious that you're there for each other. You *care* for each other.'

Martine was stunned. 'Look,' she said, 'my life might

seem perfect to you, but you wouldn't believe how many people I've managed to upset or disappoint over the past few weeks. I've even hurt Ben – the nicest person I've ever met. But, earlier this year, when the white giraffe was stolen because of something dumb I did, somebody told me it's never too late to fix things.'

Claudius gave a tired laugh. 'I'm not sure about that. Anyway, now that you know the truth about me, you can take your revenge. Go on. Tell everyone what a loser I am.'

Nathan's dark head came round the door of the shelter. He thrust forward a bamboo pole with five fat fish speared on it. 'Ta-dah!' he trumpeted. His eyes widened when he saw that Claudius was conscious. 'Is everything okay in here? We heard voices.'

'Everything's fantastic,' Martine assured him. 'Claudius has just woken up. He was wondering if anyone has had a chance to go to McDonald's yet? If not, he says some coconut milk and a fish barbecue breakfast would be perfect.'

20

The revival of Claudius changed everything. There was no longer any separation between the seven of them, and nobody suggested that there should be. It was agreed that they would all sleep on the beach until Claudius was well enough to climb the steep dunes, and then they would all stay together in the lighthouse.

Martine had spent a good proportion of her school days in solitude, and had never been involved in any team sports (vacancies on netball and hockey teams at school had an uncanny way of being conveniently full when she applied to join them), so it was a novel experience for her to be part of a group, especially since she was a very appreciated part because of what she'd done for Claudius.

'It's not me you have to thank; it's Grace,' Martine kept saying to everyone. 'She gave me the plant.'

'Yes,' said Sherilyn, 'but you guessed what the leaves were for. You kept them alive. I mean, when you put them in that bottle in our cabin, I thought you were a fruitcake.'

One of the first things Martine discovered about being in a group was that, while at school you could fool yourself into thinking you knew people really well because you saw them every day, you never actually knew them until you had to live with them.

Take Sherilyn. Martine had always thought of Sherilyn as being nice but a bit dim, and had taken it for granted that she came from a cereal-box-perfect family living behind electric gates in a suburb packed with other cereal-box-perfect families. Yet she couldn't have been more wrong. It turned out that Sherilyn's actress mum had walked out of the house when Sherilyn was one and her brother and sister were two and three, and hadn't been seen since. For the past seven years, Sherilyn had been living with her dad, siblings and Thai stepmother in one of Storm Crossing's most bohemian, multicultural neighbourhoods.

As a consequence of her step-mum's influence, she had become quite a good cook. Nobody had found that out until now because Sherilyn had spent a lot of her time on the island homesick, weeping and trying to escape from crabs and insects. Also, for the most part, there hadn't been any food for her to cook or any fire for her to cook with. Now she had both. Claudius's near-death experience had made her pull herself together and she was determined to contribute. There was limited fare on the island but Sherilyn worked wonders with what there was. It was she who recognized the grizzled old tubers in a store-cupboard in the lighthouse as cassava, a root vegetable. Jake improvised a pot for her using bulb protectors from the lighthouse. She boiled the cassava and mashed it and served it up on banana leaves, accompanied by fish cooked in coconut milk and flavoured with wild chillies, herbs and green lemons. They ate it with their hands and somehow that made it extra tasty.

The fish were provided by Nathan and Ben, their chief fishers. There wasn't too much to discover about Nathan, who was sweet but dull and would probably grow up to be an accountant, but he was very likeable and a good person to have around. He was never going to be a nature-lover, but he did enjoy fishing, and once, when he and Ben had come across a bees' nest in the hollow of an old tree, he'd unexpectedly revealed that his uncle was a beekeeper. Before anyone could stop him he was smoking the bees out of their hole. He earned a great, dripping wedge of honeycomb and two stings for his trouble.

Lucy, meanwhile, had recovered her airs and graces – something Martine found weirdly comforting. She spent a lot of time lying in the sun complaining about the stains and rips in her white tracksuit, and being nostalgic about Luke. She was nice (well, nice-ish) to Martine, but not exactly industrious. Most of her energy seemed to have been expended on the night Claudius fell ill.

'I'm so bored,' she told anyone who would listen. 'I miss TV, I miss music, I miss my room. I miss Luke and my mum and dad and my bed and soap and toothpaste and shampoo and coffee and chocolate. *Boy*, do I miss chocolate. But mostly I'm just bored. Bored, bored, bored.'

Jake had set himself the task of maintaining the giant SOS (large enough to be seen by passing aircraft) on Runway Beach. He did everything that was asked of him, effortlessly gathering great piles of wood, but he kept himself to himself. To varying degrees, they all went through parts of every day where they hated their island prison, lovely as it was, but Jake agonized most over the rugby training he was missing. He made a crude rugby ball out of coconut husk and bark, and whiled away the hours kicking it over palm trees and doing press-ups so that he'd be match-fit when he eventually returned to Storm Crossing.

Not surprisingly, Ben was the subject of much interest. Jake had not yet forgiven him for 'deceiving everyone', as he saw it, by making them think he was mute, and Lucy, who had always ridiculed him as a tree-hugging nutcase, now had to live with the remembrance of how she had treated him. But everyone was fascinated to hear his story. Not that he gave them much information. When Sherilyn asked him the question they all wanted the answer to, namely, why had he never spoken at school, Ben replied simply, 'I didn't have anything to say.'

But after years of being an outcast, he, like Martine, couldn't help but enjoy being included or asked for his opinion or help, which he frequently was. Of everyone, Ben had adapted best to island life. It was as if he was born to it. It made Martine proud to see the envious faces of kids who had always bullied or belittled him, when they saw him swim, fish, or build beds or shelters.

'Where did you learn all that?' Sherilyn wanted to know.

'All what?' Ben said, and then pretended he had an urgent appointment with Nathan on the other side of the island.

Over the next three evenings, the seven of them came together around a fire on the sea shore, and everyone except Claudius talked about the things they had in common – the dolphins, or their feelings on the night of the storm, or how desperately they missed their families, or how terrified they were of never being found, or whether or not they would do things differently when they left the island. Topics like pop music and the bizarre behaviour of celebrities, favourites at school, seemed trivial after what they'd been through.

Claudius was still too weak and listless to participate. If someone addressed him, he would nod, or shake his head, or give a one sentence answer, but most of the time he just stared into the flames.

'I never thought I'd say this,' Ben commented privately to Martine, 'but I miss the old Claudius. The spirit of him, anyway.'

Only Martine knew the root cause of Claudius's blues.

When they were alone together on the second day of his recovery, he'd mumbled something about hating himself for letting everyone down.

'I told everybody that my father would have us out of here in forty-eight hours,' he confided. 'I told them it was hard to get lost these days. I got my friends' hopes up. Now we could be stranded here for months.'

'Nobody blames you for that,' she assured him. 'Tendai always says it's important to be positive in a survival situation. Anyway, it was you getting sick that brought us all together. Don't worry. We'll be rescued soon.'

Inside she didn't feel nearly as confident as she sounded. She couldn't stop thinking about something Ben had said earlier. 'Martine, I have a really bad feeling about this island. I don't think it's a coincidence that the only boat we've seen in nearly a week is one that came to investigate an explosion. There is a reason people are staying away. There's something wrong with this place.'

It was Jake who came to tell them that the dolphins were behaving strangely.

'I was practising sprints at Dolphin Bay and they came right up to the shore. I thought it was cool that they were watching me, but then they started milling around and acting all confused. You'd better come see what's going on.'

It was late afternoon. Everyone but Claudius, who was

still too weak to leave his bamboo cot for more than a few hours at a time, ran the length of Runway Beach. They rounded the peninsula and were confronted with the most heartbreaking sight. Twenty-one dolphins were splayed across the white sand in golden sunlight. Something had driven them to flee the sea. The tide was going out and they were stranded, waiting to die.

Martine couldn't believe what she was seeing. It was the image in the cave painting, right down to the number of dolphins. The second prophecy had just come true.

But it was worse. These were the dolphins who had saved them from the ocean's wrath. They had become friends. They had names. Sun Dancer, Rain Queen, Patch, Honey, Thunder, Ash, Steel and Mini and, most distressingly, Little Storm – they were all there.

Everyone turned to Martine for answers. 'What do we do? How do we save them?' they clamoured.

Martine didn't know how to respond. Even supposing they were able to keep twenty-one dolphins from dying of shock and over-heating, which she doubted, there was no earthly way that they were strong enough to carry any dolphin apart perhaps from Little Storm to the water's edge. Not with the tide going out. The sea was retreating so quickly that it was already more than twenty feet from the nearest dolphin. Soon it would be a quarter of a mile away.

She wanted to shout back, 'Why are you asking me? I'm not a doctor or a vet. I'm an eleven-year-old kid. Yes, I have a gift, but I don't know what it does, or what it's for, or how to use it properly!'

But that wouldn't help the dolphins. Plus, she was not about to admit to having a gift. So she just said, "There's only one thing we can do and that's try to keep them wet and cool until the tide turns and we can push them back out to sea.'

'How long will that take?' Lucy asked. 'I mean, are we talking one hour? Two hours?'

'Twelve hours,' Ben told her.

Sherilyn gulped. 'Twelve hours? We're meant to keep them wet and cool for twelve hours?'

'Well, we just can't,' Lucy declared flatly. 'Simple as that. We'll be dead as well.'

'We can try,' Nathan said, but without much conviction.

Martine glanced at Ben. Precious minutes were being wasted while they argued.

'These dolphins saved our lives,' Ben reminded them.

'*Ja*,' agreed Jake, 'and if it was a matter of keeping them wet for an hour or two, I'd be the first to do it. But get real, guys. You're asking us to keep twenty-one dolphins wet for a whole day.'

'Exactly!'

They all jumped. Unnoticed, Claudius had come up behind them. He was swaying slightly and his skin was still more yellow than gold, but there was something of his old charisma in the set of his shoulders. 'That's what you do when someone, or something saves your life,' he told Jake. 'You save theirs right back. Come on everyone, you heard Martine. We need to keep the dolphins wet.'

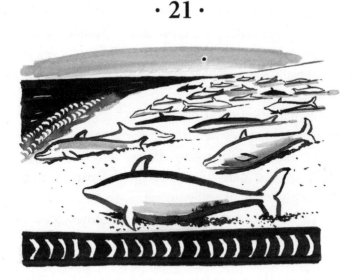

21

It was extraordinary to witness how much one not-very-well boy could do to galvanize a group. Before anybody could object, Claudius had organized Jake to run to the lighthouse and Runway Beach to collect every bulb, pot or container capable of holding water, plus some palm fronds to shade them all. Ben and Nathan were sent to gather firewood and catch fish, because, Claudius said, they would need all the energy they could get to make it through the night. Lucy and Sherilyn were dispatched to gather up the honeycomb, coconuts, spare clothing, and chunks of aloe. Martine hoped that the aloe leaf gel would help soothe the dolphins' exposed skins and prevent them from cracking.

She and Claudius stayed behind to dig holes in which to tuck the dolphins' pectoral fins, which would help keep them upright and comfortable. Then they spread great armfuls of seaweed over the dolphins to keep them from literally cooking in their own blubber. Martine went from one to the next, putting her palms over their hearts and feeling the tingle of electricity in response. They gazed up at her with their limpid, knowing eyes as if they trusted her to help them, and that terrified Martine because she was afraid she might not be able to.

And as she walked and murmured to them, not really knowing what she was saying, she became aware that what had started as a feeling of anguish when she saw the dolphins in distress, was gradually consuming her heart. It was as if they were extensions of her. When she looked into Little Storm's eyes, she saw that he recognized something she herself had never understood until that moment. That she felt his pain. She took on the burden of it.

Claudius was unaware of these internal revelations as he followed her, pausing in between dolphins to scoop up water from the departing sea with containers he'd improvised from a large shell and a coconut.

'Thanks for what you did earlier,' Martine said, as she watched him pour water onto Rain Queen's head, taking care to avoid her blow hole. If water went into the blow hole she used for breathing, she could drown.

Claudius's mouth twisted. 'No, thank *you*,' he replied. And she knew he wasn't talking about the dolphins.

When she reached Sun Dancer, Martine cradled the dolphin's silver-grey head in her arms and kissed him. Fighting back tears, she said softly, 'Please, Sun Dancer, find a way to tell us how to help you.'

'What do you expect – that he's suddenly going to start talking like Flipper?' Claudius jibed with a flash of his old sarcasm. But he knew straight away that he'd been insensitive and tried to make amends, saying, 'You really love them, don't you?'

'Yes, I do. Why, how do you feel about them?'

Claudius gave Sun Dancer's back an experimental stroke. 'I'm not sure. I haven't been around them as much as you. I just know that saving them seems like the most important thing I've ever done in my life. I care about that more than I care about getting off this island.'

But saving the dolphins was, as Jake had predicted, backbreaking work. They split into two groups and worked in shifts. Martine, Jake and Lucy took the first shift because Nathan and Ben were still out fishing. Each of them had responsibility for seven dolphins. They had to apply aloe gel to their skins, pour seawater over them and then drape them with seaweed. The most tiring part was the trips to the lake for fresh water, or to the edge of the crashing waves around the peninsula, a stony beach they'd named 'Danger', to fill the various containers Jake had found. Every hour, they switched, and slept, ate or stared into space while Ben, Nathan and Sherilyn took a turn with the dolphins. Then they'd rotate.

Claudius didn't have the stamina of the others, so it was his job to keep the fire blazing, time the shifts, motivate everyone, and attempt to cook meals, which he did extremely badly – so badly that it was decided after a disgusting lunch that at mealtimes he should take over Sherilyn's duties with the dolphins while she cooked.

As night drew in, a wicked wind whipped up the surf and the temperature plunged. They were on Danger Beach filling the containers when Ben suddenly stopped what he was doing, straightened and said, 'Did anybody hear that?'

Everyone fell silent. A wave crashed and the sea was temporarily hushed. The sound came again – a distinct ping. They waited a few seconds and it happened once more.

'That's the sound I heard when I was doing my exercises,' said Jake. 'A pinging noise. I thought it was a bird, or some weird fish or other.'

'It's sonar,' Ben told him.

'Sonar!' cried Martine.

Ben raised his eyebrows. 'Yes, sonar. When my dad was in the navy he took me to see the testing of a new transmitter, and I'd know that noise anywhere. Basically, a transmitter sends out pulses of sound that bounce off submarines and other objects in the ocean and are detected as returning echoes. That's what the ping is. But why would anybody test it out here? If we can hear it, it's probably Low-Frequency Active sonar, which is used by the navy.'

'A lot of scientists believe that LFA sonar's one of the main causes of dolphins and whales getting stranded,' said Martine, remembering her conversation with

Mr Manning during the Sardine Run.

'If scientists know that, why do the navy still use it?' Sherilyn asked.

'Grown-ups don't always fix the obvious things,' Nathan told her.

'That's because they're so busy telling us not to eat too many sweets, or run in the house, or talk to strangers, or stand under trees when there's lightning, they don't have time,' Lucy remarked.

There was quiet as they listened again for the pinging noise, but it had stopped.

'That's a pity,' said Jake. 'If there's sonar, maybe it means the navy are about and if the navy are about, they might save us and take us back to Cape Town.'

Everybody glared at him and he had the grace to look ashamed. 'I'm just *saying* . . . ' he said defiantly. 'Of course I care about the dolphins.'

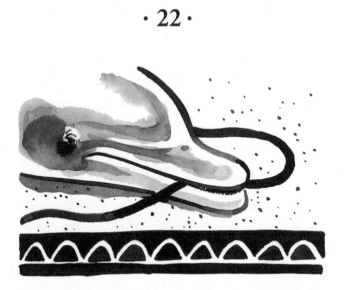

22

To be fair, Jake more than pulled his weight during the endless night that followed. It was so cold and the ritual rinsing of dolphins' skins so mind-numbing that half the time Martine wasn't sure if she was awake, asleep or hallucinating. She worried that the unaccustomed pressure could damage their kidneys, livers and hearts, so she focussed what little healing power she could summon on those organs. Once an hour, she moved from dolphin to dolphin in the fire-lit darkness, running her hands along their abdomens and bellies in such a subtle way that not even Ben noticed.

To take her mind off her muscles, which soon grew

sore to the point of screaming, she allowed her thoughts to drift to Sawubona. There was a giraffe-shaped hole in her heart where Jemmy was supposed to be. She wondered what he was doing now, and whether he missed her as much as she missed him. She wondered if she'd ever again have the chance to ride him up to onto the escarpment on a starry night, as she'd done before Gwyn Thomas stopped her from riding after sundown, and to lie with her head on his withers and her feet on his hindquarters, losing herself in Mars, the Southern Cross and the Milky Way. On those nights, she'd felt cloaked by Africa, almost as if the mother spirit of the landscape had cast a protective veil around her shoulders.

She missed Grace's wisdom and Tendai's bass-drum laugh and, increasingly, she missed the evenings with Gwyn Thomas. Sometimes her grandmother was worn out from a hard day on the reserve and they'd just sit quietly together after dinner, listening to the radio or reading books, but at other times she'd tell Martine tales of the history of Southern Africa – of rivers running red with the blood of spear-throwing Zulus and *Voortrekkers,* the early white settlers; of epic, malaria and blackwater fever-wracked journeys by oxwagon; of tribes displaced by the whims of politicians in Europe; of men driven mad with greed for gold and diamonds.

She talked, too, of Martine's mum and dad, and those were the stories Martine cherished most. 'Your mum always said that she knew David was the man for her when she watched him wade into the middle of a torrential river to rescue a baby monkey clinging to a fragment of rock,' Gwyn Thomas had told her with a smile.

David Allen was an Englishman, in Cape Town for a medical conference, and for both him and Veronica it was love at first sight. They'd been married at the game reserve, three months after David waded from the river with the dripping baby monkey, and David had moved to South Africa to be with his new bride. He'd found a job at a famous hospital, and for a while the future had looked perfect.

Until fate had intervened. Or, at least, until Grace had told Veronica that her baby – born on New Year's Day, a year after their wedding – had a gift with animals. The *sangoma* warned her that the gift would carry an awesome responsibility, and that Martine's destiny was unalterable. Those words had changed everything.

'Martine. Martine!'

Martine shook herself. Nathan was standing in front of her. 'You can rest now,' he said. 'You look as if you need it.'

In the end, the actual saving of the dolphins was almost an anti-climax. The tide came in shortly before four-thirty a.m. and left foaming outlines around the dolphins, who by then were as weak as their carers. The water took an age to inch high enough up the beach to actually lift the dolphins off the sand, and by that point nobody was capable of doing anything but encouraging them to swim out to sea.

The dolphins moved tentatively at first and then with increasing fluidity and speed. Martine's chest was tight with emotion as she watched them go, especially when Sun Dancer wheeled back and clicked to her before leaving.

'We did it!' whooped Jake. Everyone came together for a group hug which, despite their wet, clammy skins, was somehow the warmest Martine had ever had. Then they collapsed in hysterical laughter on the sand.

'That's it,' said Lucy. 'I'm officially on holiday. I refuse to lift a finger between now and when we leave the island. I don't care if we're stuck here for a year.'

'How is that different to usual?' Claudius asked drily, and even Lucy had to giggle.

All of a sudden Sherilyn said, 'Oh, no!'

Nathan groaned.

'What is it?' asked Martine. She sat up and squinted into the sunlight. Mini was on the fringe of the surf. It was plain she intended to beach herself again.

Martine was distraught. The weight of the dolphins' suffering returned to crush her again. 'Maybe she's so traumatized she's lost the will to live. That happens to some dolphins. No matter how many times they're returned to the sea, they keep trying to escape it.'

'Come on, everyone,' Claudius said tiredly, 'back to work.'

'I can't,' Lucy whined. 'I just can't.'

'Get up off your lazy bum and come and help,'

Sherilyn ordered much to everyone's astonishment, and Lucy, to her credit, did just that.

Three times they pushed Mini out to sea and three times the dolphin returned. Finally their strength really did run out. The marathon night had taken its toll.

Mini dragged herself onto the beach one final time and Martine went to sit beside her, to try to comfort her in her last moments. 'Don't you want to be in the ocean any more?' she asked despairingly. 'Don't you want to be with your friends?'

She was stroking Mini's head when she noticed something jutting from the dolphin's mouth. She removed it carefully. It was a section of clear cable.

Martine's hands began to shake. 'Ben,' she called, and he was by her side in an instant. He took the cable from her and examined it closely, and they both looked over at Mini. The grandmother dolphin's eyelids slid shut and she heaved a big sigh.

'No, Mini, you're not allowed to die,' Martine sobbed, but it was already too late.

Sherilyn came over and tried to console her, but Martine was beyond consolation. Someone, or something, had killed Mini as surely as if they had shot her, and she was not going to rest until she found out who, or what, had done it.

'I think you're right,' she said in a low voice to Ben when Sherilyn stepped away to talk to the others. 'There *is* a reason why people are staying away from this island. It's cursed, or protected, or there's a secret here. There *is* something wrong with this place. And what do the cables have to do with anything?'

'I don't know,' Ben said. 'But I know we're not going to be able to find the answers on our own.'

· 23 ·

W ho do you think the men are?' Nathan said. 'MI5 spies? Foreign mercenaries plotting a coup?'

They were up in the lighthouse, thawing out around a roaring fire. They were filthy, smelly and so sleep-deprived they practically needed matchsticks to keep their eyelids open, but the discovery that the sea around the island was a virtual minefield, and that they were not alone at all but so close to 'civilization' that men in dhows could be on the scene in minutes, had temporarily re-energized them.

'We're not sure,' Ben told him. 'They could even be pirates.'

'*Pirates?*' Lucy said skeptically. 'Are you making this up? Did they also have eye-patches and cutlasses and a black flag with a skull and crossbones on it?'

'Modern pirates aren't like that,' Nathan informed her. 'I saw a documentary on them. They prey on tourist boats and cargo vessels in isolated locations just like this one, and are so bold they'll swarm aboard in broad daylight and rob people at knifepoint. They're ruthless.'

'*Oh. My. God!* So, along with being half-drowned and marooned on an island, we're now going to be murdered by pirates?'

'Well, we don't have anything to steal,' Ben said, unable to hide a smile, 'so I don't think they'd be too interested in us, even if they are pirates. It's more likely that they're treasure hunters who've booby-trapped the wreck to keep other fortune seekers away from it, or that they're working for the organization that laid down the cables. If we're right and Mini *was* trying to tell us that there's a connection between the dolphins beaching themselves and the cables, then we need to find out what the cables are for. Especially if it turns out that the undersea mine was protecting the cables and not the wreck.'

'Why don't we take a closer look at them?' Jake suggested.

'What, and get blown to pieces like the Manta Ray?' exclaimed Lucy. 'No thanks.'

'What about the sonar?' asked Martine. 'Do you think the men we saw could be involved with that?'

'Sonar can travel for miles, so the transmitter that's

being used could be anywhere,' Ben said. 'Some navy might be testing in the middle of the Indian Ocean. Maybe we should concentrate on the divers, because they and the cables are our only clues. The fact that they responded to the explosion so rapidly means that they must be based reasonably close to us, possibly on another island – although not close enough to know that we're here. Unless it was just chance and they happened to be sailing nearby.'

'What happens if they do notice we're here?' fretted Sherilyn. 'Are they going to come to the island and shoot us with their spear-guns?'

Claudius made a scary face at her. 'No, they'll just kidnap us and hold us for ransom.'

'Well, that's a real comfort,' Lucy said sarcastically, and Martine smothered a giggle. Claudius was definitely on the mend.

'The one thing I keep thinking about is how proud Alberto was there was no crime in the Bazaruto Archipelago,' she said. 'He told me that the islanders don't even have locks on their doors and that the smallest child can walk anywhere by themselves. He didn't say anything about pirates or undersea mines. So maybe there's an innocent explanation for all of this.'

'We're forgetting the most important part of this,' Claudius interrupted, 'and that's the dolphins. I mean, we owe it to them to find and stop whatever it is that's causing them to beach themselves.'

'Why don't we start by trying to find out where the divers are operating from?' Ben suggested. 'If we can get them to come to the island, we might be able to follow them.'

'Oh, sure,' Lucy said. 'Let's just phone them up and invite them over!'

Jake snorted. '*Follow* them? In what? The raft we're going to build out of bamboo, I suppose. That's going to be really effective.'

'We'll take their boat,' Ben responded calmly.

'And how do you suppose we're going to do that?'

'Don't tell me,' said Martine, remembering something Ben had once said to her. 'Sometimes the most obvious way is the best way.'

Ben laughed. 'That's right.'

As eager as they were to get started, everyone agreed that, in order for any plan to be effective, sleep was their first priority. Claudius's water-resistant-to-200 metres watch had survived the storm, so he set his alarm for 3 p.m. That would give them four hours of rest, leaving them with three hours to execute phase one before dark.

In the event, they were awoken at 2:10 p.m. by the sound of an aeroplane. Jake heard it first. He scrambled to his feet, brown hair sticking up porcupine-style, stumbled outside, and started leaping up and down and waving his arms. Lucy and Nathan went after him and the three of them did wild dances on top of the dunes.

But the Cessna was circling Dolphin Bay and gave no indication it had seen them.

They ran back into the lighthouse and tried, in a comical way borne of haste, to restart the fire so they could send up a smoke signal. The first flames were just taking when Claudius threw water on them.

Jake snatched the gourd from him. 'Claudius, what the hell are you doing, mate? Has the man-o'-war venom attacked your brain? We've got a chance of getting off this island. Don't you want that?'

'Don't worry about it, Jake,' said Nathan. 'They'll see the SOS on Runway beach.'

Jake glared at Claudius, tossed aside the gourd, and raced outside again. The others joined him. Martine had snatched the tin lid from her survival kit, and she tilted it upwards in the hope the pilot might spot the reflected glare of the sunlight, but the plane flew past without seeming to see them. It dipped low over Runway Beach and circled twice.

'They've seen it,' yelled Jake. 'Whoooee! We're saved. We're out of here. I'm going to play rugby again. I'm going to eat steak and chips again.'

But the plane soared upwards and the drone of its engine soon dissipated in the afternoon blue.

'That's it,' Lucy declared with a loud sniff. 'I'm never going to see my twin again. We're doomed to stay here for eternity.' She slumped to the ground and put her head in her hands.

Jake raked his hands through his hair. 'I don't understand it. How could they miss our sign? It could practically be seen from Mars.' He walked to the edge of the dunes and shaded his eyes. 'Hold on a minute. It's gone. The SOS is gone!'

'Don't be a moron, Jake,' said Lucy, not bothering to raise her head. 'As if anyone would steal your stupid sign.'

'I did,' Claudius said.

Jake gave him a baffled look. 'What are you talking about?'

'I took the SOS away. I moved all the stones late last night when I went to Runway Beach to find my sweater.'

Six appalled faces turned his way. 'But why?' Nathan asked in bewilderment. 'Why would you do that?'

'It's because his rich father hasn't come to save him, and Claudius is afraid it's because his dad doesn't want his fat, bone-idle son any more,' Jake said nastily. 'He's afraid to go home.'

Sherilyn rounded on him. 'Don't be so spiteful, Jake. What's wrong with you?'

'It's true, Sherilyn,' Claudius admitted. 'I have been afraid that my dad doesn't want his fat, bone-idle son back and that that's the real reason he hasn't come looking for me. I *am* afraid of going home. But that isn't why I did it. I did it because I suddenly realized that if we were rescued too soon, we wouldn't be able to save the dolphins. I mean, if that plane had found us and we'd told whoever was on board, "Oh, by the way, we think the dolphins are beaching themselves because of sonar testing, or some weird cables, or divers who plant undersea mines, and we need to stay longer to investigate," they would have said, "In your dreams.

We're taking you back to your families right now.'''

He paused and stared hard at his fellow castaways – Jake in particular. 'We've got a chance to make a real difference here. Don't you want that? Isn't that more important than whether or not you get to play centre forward at some rugby match?'

A tense silence greeted this speech. Martine was the first to move. She went over to Claudius and stood beside him. 'What Claudius says makes sense,' she told the rest of the group. 'There's no way we'd be allowed to stay and help the dolphins if any adult found us now.'

'A few more days on the island is nothing compared to that,' agreed Ben.

Lucy gave an exasperated sigh, which Martine took as a yes – albeit a very irritated one; and Sherilyn nodded, although her lower lip wobbled.

'It's not like we have loads of other options,' Nathan reminded Jake. 'People don't seem to be in too much of a hurry to rescue us.'

Jake vented his annoyance on a piece of coconut husk which happened to find itself in front of his foot. 'All right,' he said. 'Two more days. Two more days and then the SOS is going back on the beach and this time it'll be twice the size!'

24

The plan they came up with was three-pronged. First they would attempt to trigger an explosion in order to try to lure the men on the dhow to the island; then Claudius would distract them while Ben and Martine, as the only pair willing to volunteer for the job, would sneak onto the boat, assuming that there was somewhere for them to hide. Once at the divers' headquarters, they would . . . well, they weren't exactly sure what they'd do when they got there, but their main aim was to find the cause of the dolphins' suffering and to try to make contact with the outside world.

That was the idea on paper – or at least on sand.

Claudius sketched it out on Runway Beach with a stick. As they talked, the faces of the seven classmates were grave. There was no fooling around. Everyone knew they could be venturing into the human equivalent of a shark tank.

They made, Martine thought, a motley crew. They'd had a much-needed bath in the lake, but without soap and shampoo there wasn't much improvement. They were all sunburnt or wind-blasted and much thinner, and their clothes were in a dreadful state. Sherilyn looked the most ridiculous in her faded pink pyjamas with missing buttons, but Claudius was almost as bad in tattered jeans, which hung loose on his reduced frame, and a red sweater which was unravelling at one elbow. If he wasn't still delicate following his man-o'-war encounter, Martine would have been sorely tempted to remind him how he'd taunted her for having holes in her jeans back in Cape Town. That said, anyone who saw Ben and Martine's stained T-shirts and threadbare denim shorts would have assumed they'd been castaways for a year, not ten days, and Lucy's white tracksuit was a sight.

Nathan and Jake had fared best in the clothes department. Jake's jeans and forest-green, yellow-collared Springbok rugby jersey were so hard-wearing they had barely been affected by his adventures, and, apart from a few creases, Nathan's checked blue shirt and navy blue chinos were in relatively good shape.

But none of them looked equipped to fight dolphin-killers.

It was phase one of the plan that bothered Martine

most. As the best swimmer and the only person who knew anything at all about undersea explosives – and that was only second-hand from his dad – Ben had been nominated to swim out to the wreck and fix a string to a tripwire. He insisted to Martine that it was not as dangerous as it sounded. 'If they made the trigger too sensitive, then any old fish which bumped into it would cause an explosion,' he said.

She wasn't convinced.

Nevertheless, she helped Lucy collect bark from the trees near the lake. The string in the survival kit was not long enough for their purposes, and Sherilyn worked as quickly as she could to add to it by weaving thin strands of bark together. Length was more important than strength. Regardless of what Ben said, it wouldn't take much to activate the tripwire.

At 4 p.m., they all set off for Dolphin Bay, Ben with a fat coil of stringy bark wrapped around one wrist, Jake carrying a lifejacket. Their strategy was simple. Ben would tie one end of the makeshift rope to the tripwire – assuming, of course, that he could actually find it – and the other end to the wreck. When the sun began to set, Jake would swim out to the wreck, collect the rope, carry it as far as the line would allow and then trigger the explosion. He'd return to the shore as fast as he could and hopefully be concealed by the time the boat men showed up. Then Claudius would go into action with phase two.

Martine wanted more than anyone to help the dolphins, but she was starting to think the plan was insane. These were not a couple of incompetent poachers they were up against. These were men with spear-guns. The best possible outcome was that the dhow men would turn out to be heart-of-gold fishermen, or employees of the cable company, who, once they'd heard Martine and her fellow survivors' story, would assist them in finding what was causing the dolphins to beach themselves, and afterwards return them to their families. The worst case scenario was that they really were pirates or treasure hunters from the mainland, who would not take kindly to having their plans disrupted. Who knew what would happen then?

So lost was she in thought that it wasn't until Ben was calf-deep in water and about to swim out to the wreck that she remembered what he was doing. She went tearing across the white sand, splashed up behind him and grabbed his arm. 'Don't go, Ben,' she said emotionally. 'I couldn't bear it if anything happened to you.'

Ben looked at her in surprise. 'I have to go.'

There was something very still about him, almost as though he'd been meditating.

Martine shook her head. 'No, you don't. It's madness. You could be blown up. We'll figure out some other way to help the dolphins.'

He returned her gaze steadily. 'You know what you said to me the other night . . . ?'

Martine was mortified. The guilt and shame of those excruciating hours came rushing back. She let go of his arm. 'I'm so, so sorry, Ben. I didn't mean it, I promise. I was just being stupid.'

But Ben cut her short. 'You were right about one thing. Sometimes it is important to stand up for what you believe in.'

He dived into the water and was gone.

The first phase of the plan went very smoothly – almost too smoothly. Although Martine covered her eyes and kept reliving the moment when the manta ray blew up and rained down on the sea like lava, Ben accomplished his mission in record time, and Lucy prodded her so she could see him balanced on the edge of the galleon, giving them the thumbs up.

'Easy,' he said as he waded from the turquoise water, but when he went to pick up a gourd to have a drink Martine noticed that his hands trembled so much he almost dropped it.

Next they all sat down to crab soup, which was very watery because they'd only had time to find three undernourished crabs.

'Nothing against your cooking, Sherilyn,' Lucy said, 'but if we ever get off this stupid island, I'm never going to eat another fish, crab or coconut meal in my life. And a herd of stampeding buffaloes couldn't drag me camping. I wouldn't sleep on the freezing, hard ground with bugs again if you paid me a million rand.'

The hardest part was the goodbyes. They'd been through so much together and nobody knew if they'd be separated for a few hours, a few days or for ever. Martine was doubtful that the closeness that now existed between the seven of them would continue if they ever made it back to Caracal Junior, but she did know they would always share a bond. She would always be loyal to them and stand up for them because they had come through for her on the night of the dolphin beaching. Twenty lives would not have been saved without them.

Martine felt in her pocket for the ivory dolphin Jake had given her. He'd carved it that afternoon from the kernel of a palm fruit. 'For good luck,' he'd said. Martine couldn't believe it. She'd been beginning to wonder if he had a rugby ball for a heart. To Ben, Jake had extended his hand and said gruffly, 'You're all right,' which was the closest he ever came to a compliment. Sherilyn had given them each a perfect cowry shell and a kiss on both cheeks, and Nathan had shaken their hands very formally and said, 'See you later,' as if they were tourists going out for a scenic tour of the islands and would be back in time for dinner.

Lucy had just given them a hug and said in a choked-up voice, 'If you find a phone, tell Luke I miss him . . . Don't forget about us, hey.'

Claudius refused to say goodbye, because he said that implied he was never going to see them again. They had to think positively. They would see each other in days, if not hours. Even so, he punched Martine affectionately on the arm and said, 'You'd better take care of yourself. You're not bad for an orphan.'

To which she retorted, 'You're not bad for a boy who

dresses like an orphan!' And he burst out laughing.

At sundown, Jake swam out to the wreck and set off the explosion. He raced back to the beach and joined Nathan, Lucy and Sherilyn up on the ledges above Dolphin Bay. Ben and Martine concealed themselves among the rocks near the shore. They had bits of coconut in their pockets in case they had to go without food for a while, but Martine had left her survival kit with the others. If the plan worked they'd hopefully be reunited soon, but in the meantime the knife, torch and other contents of the kit were essential for island-living. All Martine had taken from it was the root ginger, in case of seasickness.

For twenty minutes nothing happened. The horizon stayed empty. Martine grew anxious. She tried to remind herself that the risk they were taking might save their lives and hurry her home to Jemmy and her friends at Sawubona, but her doubts soon overwhelmed her. Her biggest terror was that there would be room on the dhow for only one of them, and that Ben would disappear into the blue and she'd have no way of knowing what had become of him.

'If we can't go together, I don't think we should do it at all,' she said, standing up and shaking the pins and needles out of her legs. 'It's too dangerous. We should stay here and think of some other way to get rescued and help the dolphins.'

Ben looked up at her. 'What if no one ever comes?'

High on the rocky ledge, Nathan made 'get down' hand signals. Martine dropped to the sand. But it was not the dhow which appeared around the side of the island, it was a motorboat. This time there were only three Africans on board, one in a diving suit. They swooshed to a stop near the wreck.

Phase two of the plan was about to go into operation.

25

Claudius had been vague about how exactly he was going to attract the attention of the boatmen, except to say that he'd confuse them with a combination of animal noises and Martine's whistle. 'They'll think they're hearing things,' he explained. 'They'll come to the island to look around but I'll hide really well and be quiet as soon as I see Martine and Ben are safely on board. As long as they don't go to Runway Beach and see our shelter, they won't suspect a thing.'

But that's not what happened at all. Five minutes after the men on the motorboat appeared, Claudius strolled onto the beach and stood in the middle of it in plain view. He had put on his red jumper and rolled up the bottoms of his jeans.

'What is he *doing*?' Martine whispered to Ben. 'He's going to get himself killed.'

Nathan and the others emerged briefly from the shadows of the ledge and called down to him to stop being so crazy and get off the beach immediately, but Claudius pretended he didn't hear them. He took out the whistle Martine had given him and blew three blasts on it. The silhouettes in the boat were thrown into a state of extreme agitation. Pulling the diver back on board, they zoomed to the shore. They gestured for Claudius to come over, but he remained anchored to the spot, waving his arms like a drowning swimmer, until they were forced to leave the boat and go to him.

'Boy, am I glad to see you!' he cried as they approached. 'I thought I was going to be stuck here until I starved to death or grew a long, grey beard.'

He thrust out a hand. 'I'm Claudius. Pleased to meet you.'

'What are you doing here?' barked the boat skipper, a gaunt man with bulging eyes and long, sinewy arms. He made no attempt to take Claudius's outstretched hand. 'How did you get here? Nobody is allowed on this island. *Nobody*. Every boat captain in Mozambique knows that. Every lodge and tour operator knows that.'

'Well, to be honest that was mentioned to us . . . '

'*Us?*' demanded the man. 'Where are the others? How many of you are here?'

'I was just getting to that,' said Claudius, as if he was

oblivious to the threatening advance of the other men. 'They abandoned me. Not on purpose, I'm sure – at least, I hope not, ha, ha – but you know what grown-ups are like when they've had a few beers. I went for a walk up to the lighthouse and returned to find them gone. I'm sure they'll be back, but I'm getting very hungry so I'm really glad you've come. Is there any chance you could give me a lift to the lodge at Benguerra?'

'This is very bad news for you and very bad news for us,' the skipper said, ignoring the question. 'No one comes near Dugong.'

'Dugong?'

'Dugong Island. This is where you are trespassing.'

Down on the shore, Ben and Martine slipped like wraiths onto the motorboat. There was a storage locker under the wheel. They dived in and shut the doors behind them. The space was cramped, wet and stunk of fish and petrol fumes, but they'd done it and they were together.

'Don't worry,' Claudius was saying to the skipper in the same confident, light-hearted tone, 'the people who brought me here will be hearing from my father. Anyway, what's so special about this place? Why is no one allowed to come here? What were you looking for out by the wreck? Are you salvage experts, or from the army or something?'

'There is a saying in English, no? Curiosity killed the pussycat.'

'Fine,' said Claudius. 'I'll just wait here until my friends come back.'

'You must hope that your friends don't come back,' the skipper advised. 'We have put . . . measures . . . around the island to keep people away. You are lucky that you and your tourist friends did not get a big surprise.' He mimicked the sound of a bomb blast and followed it with a gap-toothed grin. His companions laughed.

The diver made a comment in Portuguese. The skipper's retort brought more laughter.

'Carlos thinks he has seen you somewhere before,' he told Claudius. 'Maybe on TV. I told him that, with your long yellow hair, it must have been a story about a princess. One who didn't like to take baths.'

'That's funny,' Claudius said amiably. 'You're funny. Anyway, it's been nice talking to you. I'm sure someone will be along to collect me. Goodbye.'

The skipper shot out a lanky arm and seized Claudius by the sleeve of his jumper. The smile left his face. 'Not so fast, my friend,' he said.

'What are you doing?' demanded Claudius, his voice rising. 'Leave me alone.'

But the man retained his grip on Claudius's sleeve. He said something to his companions, and they moved in a bit closer. The diver seized his other arm.

'It is not the island way to refuse hospitality to a stranger,' the skipper said coldly. 'We must not leave you here. If you please, you will accompany us to Paradise.'

Inside the dark compartment, Martine and Ben heard only snatches of what was said, but enough to gather that Claudius was more or less being kidnapped. He was still protesting, although not particularly convincingly, when the motor roared to life and the boat cruised out towards the open sea. To Martine, it sounded as if he wanted to go with the men. She was quite sure that that had been his intention all along.

As the boat picked up speed and hit rolling ocean swells, she and Ben were thrown around bruisingly. There was nothing beneath them but an anchor and a coil of wet, stiff rope, which made an extremely uncomfortable cushion and which they hoped would not be required when they reached their destination. Dirty water swilled around their space. Petrol fumes floated in. Disoriented, Martine began to feel seasick. Within minutes it was so bad she was convinced that she would vomit and the retching sounds would get them caught. But Ben produced the piece of ginger and insisted she eat it. She sucked on the fiery root and the nausea retreated, although it didn't go away altogether.

It was difficult to hear anything above the roar of the motor and the pounding of the hull against the waves, and the men didn't speak much. Martine kept her spirits up by telling herself that every mile might be taking her nearer to Jemmy and Grace and her grandmother and Tendai, but the journey seemed interminable. Plus there was the knowledge that every mile might really be taking her further away from her loved ones. It was abundantly clear that the men were not friendly fishermen or good-natured islanders. They were up to something. They had as good as admitted that Dugong Island was booby-trapped to keep people away. So what were they hiding? And where did that leave her, Ben and Claudius – or, for that matter, their friends still stuck on the island?

Her thoughts were interrupted by the slowing of the boat. The engine was switched off. They drifted on the tide until the boat bumped into land. It rocked as the men jumped out. Attempts were made to pull it out of the water, but then the movement stopped and the diver could be heard grumbling.

'Carlos is complaining that the boat feels very heavy tonight. It must be you,' the skipper said rudely to Claudius. 'Get off.'

Sand scraped loudly beneath the fibreglass hull as the boat was dragged further up onto the beach. At last, to Martine's immense relief, it was still.

'Welcome to Santa Carolina,' announced the skipper, as though Claudius were a carefree holidaymaker and not a virtual prisoner. 'A lot of people call it Paradise Island, but that will not be you, I think.'

26

Martine and Ben stayed where they were for as long as they could stand it, which was only about another ten minutes because the stench of petrol and the claustrophobia brought on by the damp compartment drove them out. Fortunately, it was early evening and there was no one around. They hopped onto the sand and stood inhaling the clean, salty smell of the ocean, which was pure heaven after the hell of their journey. A long, white beach tailed away, lit by the dim glow of the rising moon. The dhow was moored midway along it. In the distance was the outline of what looked to be a low, sprawling hotel or holiday apartments.

'Maybe it's one of those luxury lodges Lucy was going on about!' Martine said hopefully. Her mind was already racing ahead to the moment when a kindly hotel manager would, after learning of their plight, offer them free accommodation for the night and allow them to phone home. She imagined herself wallowing neck-deep in a bubble-bath before tucking into a dinner of roast chicken, crispy potatoes and loads of fresh vegetables, smothered in gravy, followed by coffee and maybe a trifle. Afterwards, she'd fall into a feather-soft bed and sleep for twenty-four hours.

'Better not get too excited,' cautioned Ben. 'They might not be pirates, but those men didn't exactly behave like hotel employees.'

'They could just be using the island as a base for their operations and have nothing to do with the hotel,' Martine said, determined not to let go of her vision. 'The hotel owner might be very interested to know that there are child kidnappers living on Paradise.'

They set off towards the buildings, the sand squeaking under their bare feet. The island was about half the size of Dugong, with gentle undulations rather than steep dunes, so they decided to follow the glittering black sea all the way round and approach the building from the back. That way they could be sure that the sinister men weren't in sight before showing themselves.

'For a hotel, there don't seem to be too many lights on,' Ben commented, as they peered between the wind-twisted trunks of some pine trees some thirty minutes later.

'It is winter in Mozambique,' Martine pointed out. 'Perhaps there are very few guests at this time of the year, or perhaps they're all at dinner.'

They waited a little while longer before venturing out into the open. It was only then, gazing up at the double-storey block of rooms and the forbidding façade of the hotel itself, its vast, curving terrace suspended over the ocean, they saw that that's all it was: a façade. A ruined shell. Not only was it unoccupied, it looked as if it had been that way for at least thirty years. The civil war or something else – mismanagement perhaps – had driven away the tourists.

Martine didn't know whether to cry or fly into a rage born of total despair. For eleven days she and the others had been trying to escape their island prison, only to end up here: the penal colony Alberto had told her about. She could still hear him saying, 'Over the years, Santa Carolina has been a playground for wealthy tourists. They call it Paradise, but oh, Miss Martine, if only they knew what that paradise had seen: hundreds of hungry, suffering prisoners, tormented beyond what any man could endure, then taken to Death Island to be swallowed by the sea.'

Martine had recounted this story to Ben on the way over. But although he had been braced for the unexpected, and hadn't allowed himself to be carried away with fantasies of feather beds or roast chicken dinners, shock was written all over his face.

'Is this what grown-ups mean when they say "Out of the frying pan and into the fire"?' Martine said.

Ben recovered sufficiently to speak. 'We're still better

off than we were,' he said. 'If there are people here – even if they do turn out to be criminals – there must also be food and some way of contacting the outside world. But no matter what, we need to be off this island by sunrise. I'm pretty sure I could sail the dhow. We'll try to rescue Claudius but if we can't we'll have to leave him and go for help. We'll be no use to him, the dolphins or anyone else if we get caught.'

Martine agreed wholeheartedly – particularly with the part about them leaving Paradise before sunrise, so they resumed their search of the hotel grounds with more urgency. The rooms they saw were all empty, their cracked walls and exposed electricity wires oddly clean, as if they were soon to be put back to use. Most eerie of all was the old ballroom, a sad shadow of its past glory. A weather-beaten, out-of-tune piano still stood in one corner, and Martine could almost hear the tinkle of keys and see the sequin-gowned dancers who must have glided across the floor beneath a brilliant chandelier. Out on the terrace, a gaping chunk of floor was missing and the sea slurped and sucked at the crumbling foundations below.

The next block of rooms was also disused, but close to the beach where they'd come in they could see lights shining among the palms. The two areas were separated by a walkway which ran almost the width of the island. A flagless pole was in the centre of it, and it was lined with weed-filled concrete flower beds in which roses or island flowers must once have bloomed. Martine and Ben were about to dart across the unkempt expanse when a lone guard appeared. He was swinging his truncheon and singing an African song in a low, sad voice. When the light fell on his face, it was young and handsome. He strolled the length of the walkway and disappeared through the palms onto the beach.

'Now!' said Ben, and they sprinted for a flat-roofed building in the centre of the grounds. For the first time in ten days, they were close to human habitation. The windows of the rooms glowed yellow, and there was washing hanging on the line. Smoke and the smell of cooking came from the rear.

They followed the sound of voices to a side window, across which a cloth had been pinned in lieu of curtains. The window was slightly ajar and the cloth hung crookedly, leaving a gap in one corner. Martine and Ben stood on tiptoe so they could see the occupants of what must have once been a dining room or restaurant. Four men were gathered around a wooden table laid with dishes of steaming food. A grainy television flickered in the background. Three of the men were eating and watching the skipper, who was up out of his seat and seemed to be tormenting a fifth person by shoving a plate of prawns and rice at them and then withdrawing it and eating a forkful himself. He stepped back and Martine had to bite her lip to keep from crying out.

Claudius was roped to a chair!

'You're lying,' the skipper was accusing him. 'You are an island spy. Who sent you?'

'Look, I would love to tell you I was a spy if it meant you'd give me some food,' said Claudius, his eyes following the prawns longingly, 'but I'm just an ordinary kid from Cape Town. How many times do I have to tell you that?'

The plate swept under his nose again and Claudius's eyes closed momentarily with the effort of resisting it. He swallowed.

Out in the cold night, Martine swallowed in sympathy.

'Was it Nico from Benguerra?' demanded the skipper. 'He is always trying to keep people from the mainland from coming in and making money from the islands. Those island grandfathers do not understand business. Their heads are in the past. We have a boy working for us, Fernando, from Bazaruto Island. He is just eighteen, but he understands that a person must take opportunities when they come, and stop worrying so much about preserving animals and plants. He is a young man with ambition. He has some things to learn about the world, but he . . . '

Behind him, Carlos let out a strangled squawk. He sprang out of his chair, gave the television two hard thumps and turned up the volume. Distorted sound blared into the room. The picture cleared slightly and the words *Sea Kestrel* Mystery – 11th day, appeared beneath a photo of Claudius. He was younger, plumper and paler, and he was wearing his old jokers' smile, but it was unmistakably him.

'Ah! Ah!' was the skipper's incredulous response, as he looked from the TV to Claudius and back again. The other men reacted the same way.

'Good evening,' intoned the newsreader. 'Eleven nights ago, seven Cape Town schoolchildren fell overboard during a freak storm off the Mozambique coast and have been missing, presumed drowned, ever since. Presumed drowned, that is, by almost everyone except property magnate Ed Rapier, father of Claudius . . . '

Martine watched Claudius turn white.

'The search has been concentrated on the Southern coastline around Inhambane where, marine experts say, currents would have carried the children in the unlikely event they survived the sharks and freezing water temperatures, and Mr Rapier has personally sponsored one of the largest air and sea rescues ever undertaken in these waters. Despite that, not a trace of the seven has been found. Yet Mr Rapier, one of South Africa's most successful businessmen, has refused to accept defeat.'

A broad-shouldered man with a grey-streaked, lion's mane of hair appeared on the screen. He was standing beside a rescue helicopter on a windy beach.

'I don't believe my boy is dead,' he told the camera. 'I will never believe it until I see his body. He is too full of life, too smart and too used to having his own way! He is a survivor. If I have to sift every grain of sand on every beach in Mozambique, I'll find him. I will never give up – and I'm sure my feelings are shared by the families of the other missing children. On their behalf, I am prepared to offer a million rand for information leading to the safe return of my son and any of his classmates.'

A contact number appeared on the bottom of the screen.

'Liar!' roared the skipper, and he struck Claudius across the face. A palm print appeared on the boy's cheek. 'You think you can talk rubbish to us and get away with it? Who else is on Dugong Island? If your friends cause trouble with the test tomorrow, I will feed you to the sharks.'

Claudius lifted his chin a fraction. There was a wobble in his voice and his fingers gripped the arms of the chair very tightly, but there was a light in his eyes that hadn't been there for days and he said determinedly, 'I was alone on the island. Completely alone. I think I must have been the only survivor. I remember getting into an empty lifeboat, but everything after that is a blur. When I woke up I was on Dugong Island. 'Course I didn't know it was called Dugong.'

This latest untruth caused the skipper to lose his temper. He slammed down the plate and lifted his arm as if to strike Claudius. A babble of furious African voices shattered the evening quiet.

The dialect they spoke was not dissimilar to Zulu, so Ben translated in a low voice. 'They are very angry with him,' he reported. 'They say he is not thinking clearly. What is he doing hitting a tourist? Here they have a chance to earn a million rand in reward money for handing over a boy who is very annoying and only going to cause trouble for them, and he is more worried about being loyal to their boss. They say he has been blinded by their boss's power. Can't he see that they are being cheated over the money from the tests? Why else does he think their boss drives a Mercedes when their own cars and bicycles are held together with string?'

The skipper seemed startled by this mutiny. He made a few feeble objections but quickly came to the conclusion they were right. They *were* being cheated. What possible harm could it do if they returned the boy and claimed the reward money for themselves? Was it not their due after all the months they'd spent caretaking Dugong Island, and been bored half to death on Paradise Island? And nobody but the four of them need know anything about it.

He smiled his gap-toothed smile. The other three smiled back. Then he untied Claudius, made a big fuss of dusting him down and straightening his clothes, and shouted to some unseen person to bring him a Coke and a hot plate of prawns and rice. 'My friend, forgive us this small misunderstanding,' he said in English. 'We are paranoid because of some problems with the islanders. Eat now and be happy. Tomorrow we will take you home to your father.'

27

The men left the room then, locking the door behind them. 'For your own safety,' the skipper told Claudius with a hyena grin. He had given him a blanket and virtually ordered him to use a torn sofa with protruding springs as a bed. After they'd gone, Martine and Ben had to wait an age for the cook to finish in the kitchen. It was only after he, too, had departed, a flick of a switch plunging the building into darkness, that they returned to the window. There were burglar bars across it, so they hissed to Claudius through the opening.

Claudius almost had a heart attack, but soon recovered and rushed over to the window. 'Ben, Martine, thank goodness you guys are here. Whatever happens, don't let anyone catch you. That skipper is nuts. Somehow you've got to try to stop them. I'm not sure what's going on, but they keep talking about a test tomorrow at noon. I haven't been able to find out what's being tested, or who is doing the testing, but it might have something to do with the dolphins.'

'What about you?' Ben whispered. 'Don't you want us to try to get you out first?'

'Are you kidding?' Claudius said. 'What, and run around chasing lunatics when I could just rest on this broken sofa, eat prawn dinners and wait to be returned to my family? No thanks. If somebody brought me a cheeseburger, I'd be in paradise. Oh, I forgot, I am in Paradise! Just go. You don't have much time.'

'Okay,' Ben said uncertainly. 'You were great, by the way.'

'Awesome,' agreed Martine.

Claudius smiled. 'Thanks.'

'Hey, Claudius . . . ' she added.

'Yeah?'

'The kidnapping story beats the yacht story hands down.'

Their first lucky break was finding that the door through which the skipper and his cronies had exited was unlocked. Their second was discovering that it led to a dark kitchen. Judging by the number of cockroaches which scuttled for cover when they walked in, it wasn't a particularly clean one, but they were too hungry to care. Inside the fridge were two big plastic bowls containing cold rice and spicy beans. Aside from a jar of pickled onions, there wasn't much else. The island menu seemed to be a combination of fish caught daily and meat from the freezer humming in the corner.

Martine and Ben fell upon the cold rice and beans and devoured the lot with gusto. It wasn't the roast chicken dinner Martine had been dreaming of, but it was edible and made a pleasant change from the fishy fare on Dugong Island. They finished off the meal with a tin of guavas which had been left out on the bench.

'What do you think we should do now?' Martine asked, wiping guava syrup from her mouth. A grease-smeared clock on the oven showed that it was coming up to ten p.m.

'Look for evidence and a phone,' Ben said. 'If they're working on a project or dealing with tests, they must have some kind of office.'

They tucked the bowls, utensils and guava tin in a cupboard where they couldn't easily be found, and padded silently through the other rooms. Their eyes had adjusted to the darkness and here and there the moonlight offered some illumination. They found a lopsided ping pong table in one room and, in the other, ceiling-high stacks of cardboard boxes with Marlin Communications written crudely on the side in black ink. A stack of copper piping was propped against the doorframe.

Ben levered open one of the boxes. It was filled with nuts and bolts, wire and fuse boxes. He opened three more, each duller than the last.

'Nothing here,' he said. 'It could be that they're ordinary communications or construction workers, and the test they were talking about has something to do with their project. It could be that they're just not very nice people.'

They looked at each other. Then both of them went, 'Nah!'

'Ordinary workers don't have undersea explosives,' Martine reminded him. 'And they don't lock up innocent children.'

'We've got two mysteries to solve,' said Ben. 'Number one, why are these men so determined to keep people away from Dugong Island? Two, who or what is killing the dolphins?'

'And are those things linked in some way?'

'Come on,' said Ben, 'we'd better hurry if we're going to find the answers by morning.'

They already knew that the dining area where Claudius was being held was a phone-free zone, so the office, if indeed there was one, was either in the staff apartments near the beach, where they'd seen the men heading, or in one of the ruined buildings. Since the staff quarters were inaccessible, they decided to start with the blocks of rooms, taking along the torch they'd found in the cutlery drawer in the kitchen. They didn't dare switch it on, but pocketed it anyway in case of emergencies.

'It's like an abandoned film set,' Martine said when they reached the ballroom after a lightning search of the rest of the hotel – a task made easier because many of the rooms were missing doors or windows. 'It's as if a plague or some terrible catastrophe has swept away all the actors and dancers.'

They stood on the terrace, breathing in the salty night air and listening to the rhythmic swish, swish of the sea. It was hard to believe that it was only yesterday that they'd stayed up till dawn trying to save the beached dolphins.

Martine yawned. 'I'm so tired,' she said. 'I feel like we've been awake for days.'

'That's because we have,' was Ben's dry reply.

A sweeping yellow beam sent them diving for cover. They'd temporarily forgotten about the guard. They crawled back into the ballroom and hid behind the piano. After a while they heard his footsteps retreating.

'We'll have to think of a way to get in to the staff apartments,' Ben said. 'There's nothing here.'

Martine put her hand on his arm. 'Wait. We haven't looked upstairs.'

'It's probably just a bar or lounge area. The whole hotel is empty. The bar is not going to be any different.'

Martine's gaze followed the curve of the spiral staircase high into the black darkness of the upper floor. It looked like the last refuge of the ghosts of Paradise

Island's penal colony, the prisoners who'd lived or died in torment centuries before the sunseekers arrived to lounge beside the ocean, or twirl beneath the twinkly lights on the ballroom floor.

'We have to be sure,' she said. 'What if it *is* different?'

The second-storey was, as Ben had suspected, a bar and lounge, but he was wrong about it being empty. Big plastic bundles lined one wall and there was a desk and a filing cabinet in front of the windows. Moonlight spilled in, but it wasn't bright enough for their purposes. They needed the torch if their hunt was to be effective. After several long minutes studying the grounds below for any sign of life, they decided to risk switching it on. The first thing they saw was the contents of the clear plastic bundles.

'The cables!' exclaimed Martine.

'So maybe we are on the right track after all,' Ben said.

But the filing cabinets were as dreary as the boxes had been over in the restaurant area. Whatever else the men were doing, their record keeping could not be faulted. Not if the neatness of their handwriting was anything to go by. File after file revealed nothing more riveting than orders for cement, and letters from the planning department reporting delays to building work.

'I guess if there was anything important here, the door would be locked,' Ben said disappointedly. 'Their computers, phones and radios are probably in their apartments.'

They were just about to leave when Martine spotted a wire basket beneath the desk. Ben handed her the torch and she moved the chair and grabbed it. Inside was a single ball of paper. She smoothed it out. It was a print-out of an email. The sender's address had been torn off but the message was still intact.

Dear M, Thank you for your kind permission to conduct a further test near Dugong Island on the date agreed. Please be advised that it will take place at 12:00hrs and will be 235 decibels. Payment is as before. VS

'Sonar testing,' said Ben, crouching down beside her. 'Has to be. What else could they be testing that's measured in decibels? Somehow these guys have got mixed up in it.'

Martine looked at the printout again. 'It doesn't have a date on it, but it could be the test that Claudius was telling us about. That means we have until noon tomorrow to stop it. Or is it today already? Do you think it's past midnight?'

She turned off the torch. 'Oh, Ben, the test that drove the whales to their deaths in the Bahamas was 235 decibels. I remember that because those are the first three digits of our phone number at Sawubona. Under water, 235 decibels sounds like a rocket taking off.'

'If it's true about the test, we're in way over our heads,' Ben said. 'We have to find a phone or a radio and get a message to my father's ship. If we can reach him, he'll contact the coastguard or the navy. We're going to need some outside help.'

Keeping low, they crept over to the arched doorway. Ben put a finger to his lips. 'Shh! Did you hear that?'

'Hear what?' whispered Martine, but by then a hand was descending from the darkness like a club, mashing her face into the floor and wrenching her arm behind her back, and it was already way too late.

· 28 ·

At least we tried,' Martine said. 'We did everything we possibly could.'

'Yes,' Ben agreed. 'We did our best.'

'We're just kids. It wasn't realistic to think that we could outwit the kind of men who blow up manta rays, 'specially not here, on some island in the middle of nowhere.'

'You're right. We're just kids.'

'It's just that . . . .' Martine's tone was wistful. 'It's just that I keep thinking, what if we'd done things differently? What if we hadn't been caught? What if we still had a chance of saving the dolphins? I can't bear to think of the agony they'll be in if the test goes ahead.'

'I know,' said Ben. 'Unless we can escape and prevent it, I feel as if we'll have failed Cookie and Sun Dancer and the others. I keep thinking that there has to still be a way to keep our promise to Mini.'

It was hard not to feel regretful. They'd had a chance and it had slipped through their fingers like sand.

After capturing them with the help of Fernando, the young guard, the skipper had turned ugly. He'd ranted that Claudius had, as he'd suspected, been lying to him about being alone on the island. He'd said that 'Claudies', as he called Claudius, would be punished – 'but not too much, because we don't want to make the father cross.'

Alarmed, Martine and Ben had insisted that Claudius had in a way been telling the truth because none of them got along. 'When we reached the island, sir, the first thing he did was tell us to get lost,' Ben had informed him.

Unfortunately, that had backfired because the skipper saw an opportunity to get even more extra cash. He would deliver Claudius to his father in the morning but would hold on to Ben and Martine for another few days and try to claim some reward money from their families. Martine noticed that he was careful not to mention the million rand he aimed to extract from Mr Rapier in front of the guard.

That's when she said, 'Why do you need more money? Aren't you getting enough from the tests?'

The skipper reacted as if he had just received several hundred volts in the rear from a cattle prod.

'What do you know about the tests?' he shouted.

'We know everything,' Martine bluffed. 'We even know that there's one tomorrow at noon. The islanders are not going to be happy when they find out what you're up to.'

If looks could kill, the skipper's would have incinerated her. Instead he shouted, 'Lock them up, Fernando. I must think of what to do with them.'

Martine and Ben's big chance came a few minutes after that. It happened when they were fumbling around in the dark for the torch and Ben found a hard, heavy object. Martine found the torch shortly afterwards and she switched it on.

Ben gave an amazed laugh. 'I don't believe it. The guard must have dropped this in the struggle. Martine, he dropped his radio!'

In the distance, Martine caught the ring of boots on concrete. 'Ben, someone's coming!'

But Ben was already adjusting the dial and putting his mouth to the microphone. 'This is Dumisani Khumalo's son, Ben, to the *Aurora*. Do you copy?'

There was no reply.

'This is Ben Khumalo to the *Aurora*. Do you read me?' he repeated.

'Ben!' said Martine. 'We're going to be caught!'

He continued without a pause. 'I can't hear you but I'm just going to hope you can hear me. Over,' he said clearly into the radio. 'At 12:00 hours tomorrow, there's going to be a 235 decibel sonar test near Dugong Island in the Bazaruto Archipelago. Over. There is a possibility that dozens of dolphins might beach themselves because of it. Over. Dad, if you get this message, Martine,

Claudius Rapier and I are on Paradise Island – Santa Carolina – and we're fine, although if you could rescue us after you've helped the dolphins, that would be great. Over and out.'

Nothing happened.

'Do you copy, *Aurora*?' Ben said desperately into the radio. 'Did you read any of that?'

As if to tease him, static crackled and hissed.

A key turned in the lock and the door burst open. A swinging gas lamp showed the panicked face of Fernando, who was carrying blankets and a bottle of water. He looked a little less fraught when he saw them sitting innocently on the windowsill, and gave a visible sigh when he caught sight of the radio, half hidden beneath the desk. Even so, he stared at them suspiciously.

'Lucky for you that you didn't find this,' he said, flinging down his load and snatching up the radio.

'Lucky for you, you mean,' Martine retorted. 'Why are you mixed up in this, anyway? You're Tsonga, aren't you? You're an islander. How can you take money from people who put bombs in the water around your beautiful home? People who murder dolphins? Those dolphins have saved generations of your fishermen.'

'What are you talking about?' he said angrily. 'Nobody is murdering dolphins. They are here to build a hotel, which will bring work to many islanders.'

'Are you sure?' Martine asked him. 'Or maybe they'll just give the work to people from the mainland. As for the tests, what do you think they're for?'

'You are a child and you are not from Bazaruto,' he said. 'You know nothing.'

The door slammed shut and he was gone.

Martine turned to Ben, who'd been quiet throughout this exchange. His knees were scrunched up and he had his face buried in his arms.

'Ben,' she said worriedly. 'Ben, what's wrong?'

But he was too distraught to reply. He kept his head down and spoke so softly that she had to lean close to him to make out what he was saying. 'They couldn't hear me. It didn't get through. The message didn't get through.'

Five-thirty a.m. found them leaning against the sacks of plastic cables, wrapped in blankets, watching the morning star flicker against the fading blue of night. For days they'd yearned for sleep, and now that it was an option – their only option in fact – they were too tired, too hungry and too concerned about what would happen next, to surrender to it.

For the first time since the dolphins had deposited them on Dugong Island, Martine was losing hope that she'd ever return to Sawubona. She thought about the last dawn she'd watched at the game reserve, twenty-four hours before boarding the bus for the school trip. Her grandmother had perched on the side of her bed and watched her with wry affection as Martine propped herself up and looked out at the elephants drinking from the misty waterhole. She could still recall the thrill she'd felt that the game reserve was her home. She'd had no idea then that her home was about to slip away from her, just as the *Sea Kestrel* had slipped away from the continent of Africa. That the sunrise she watched might be the last she ever saw at Sawubona.

'Ben,' she said. 'Do you mind if I ask you a question? Just in case . . . You know, just in case . . . '

He smiled wearily. 'Just in case you're too busy to ask me when we make it back to Cape Town, you mean? Sure. What do you want to know?'

'Why don't you ever speak at school?'

'Promise you won't laugh.'

'Promise.'

'A long time ago I read this Buddhist quote: "Say nothing that doesn't improve on silence." I guess it just . . . '

There was a jingle of keys and the door flew open. Fernando rushed in. 'I can't find the key for the motorboat,' he said. 'Can you sail?'

Ben and Martine tore through the coconut groves to the beach, but their strength was depleted and every stride was an effort. When Martine's feet came into contact with the cold, squeaking sand, she almost collapsed. Her arm was still sore where it had been wrenched by the skipper, she had a stitch in her side and her legs felt like two tree stumps. A large part of her just wanted to give up; lie down on the beach, go to sleep and hope that when she woke up, somebody else would have saved the day. She forced herself on, telling herself that she was running to save the dolphins. Running to get back to Jemmy. Running to be reunited with her grandmother, Grace, Tendai and the sanctuary animals at Sawubona.

'Follow the sun and you'll reach my home island, Bazaruto,' Fernando had promised. 'Somebody there will help you, for sure.'

At first they'd just stood stock still and stared at him, like birds unexpectedly released from a cage.

'You want to know why, don't you?' he said. 'It's because when you spoke to me last night, it reminded me that I went to the mainland to find honest work – to better myself – not to lock up children or work for people who would cause the *mathahi*, the dolphins, to die. So it is time to look for a different job.' He grinned. 'Anyway, I am a terrible guard.'

They'd thanked him profusely and sped off, but as they neared the water, they could see that escaping wasn't going to be quite as easy as it sounded. It wasn't just that there was very little wind. There was no breeze at all. Without it, the dhow was going nowhere.

Ben didn't hesitate. 'We'll take the motorboat.'

'*How?* We don't have a key,' said a frantic Martine, but Ben was already on his way over to the sleek white vessel. He leapt on board. Martine followed more slowly.

'Keep a look out,' Ben told her. 'I'm going to try to start it manually. A lot of boats have a hand crank as a back up.'

This boat did, too, just not a very cooperative one. Time and time again Ben tugged at the cord, but the most he could get out of it was a feeble cough. He paused, panting, for a breather.

Martine was a nervous wreck. 'Let me try,' she said impatiently, leaving her post. She wrenched with all her strength at the cord and the engine roared to life.

'You've done it!' Ben cried in disbelief. 'Martine, you're a star.'

There was a thud and the boat rocked violently. They both swung around.

'Going somewhere?' enquired the skipper.

· 29 ·

To Martine, there was a certain symmetry to the whole island adventure. An inevitability. It was almost as if destiny had been in motion since the day Miss Volkner had told them about the Sardine Run, and that no matter how hard Martine had tried to stop it, she was always going to end up speeding across the ocean on a boat steered by a man with only one purpose: to deliver her to Death Island. And she knew without being told that that's where she and Ben were being taken.

'Are you really going to leave us here to die?' she demanded when the boat spluttered to a halt at a shell sandbank and the skipper indicated that they should get off. When she hesitated, he gave her a push.

'What kind of monster are you?' she said furiously.

'Monster? I'm not a monster. If I was, I would have fed you to the sharks. No, I am a kind man – a generous man – as you will see. I am giving you a chance to win your freedom, like the old prison guards used to. You are young and strong. If you can swim to the shore, just eight miles from here, you can go home to your families, and I will forget that you tried to steal my boat and interfere with my business and stop my chance to get some real money. A million rand. Do you know how much that can buy in Mozambique?'

He revved up the engine. 'Enjoy your swim,' he said. 'Perhaps if you are lucky, a fishing boat will come to your aid.' He was gone in a swoosh of flying spray.

Martine looked at the sliver of sandbank and the seething ocean that surrounded it. Her nightmares returned in flashback. She could hear the screams on the night of the storm; feel the slow-motion terror of impending disaster; see the circling, dead-eyed sharks. She knew now how the Paradise Island prisoners must have felt in centuries gone by. At least she could swim a little; most of them had probably been unable to swim at all.

Ben was scared, too, although he was trying hard not to show it. He said, 'I don't suppose one of your powers is holding back the tide? No? Well, hopefully a fishing boat really will come along and rescue us. Until then, why don't we pretend we're on a lovely beach and that we've chosen to be here? I could help you with your sea swimming if you like.'

Martine appreciated the effort, but couldn't bring herself to go along with it. She tried to muster a smile. 'I'd really like you to give me swimming lessons sometime, but it would be nice if it was on a Cape Town beach in the summer, not Death Island in the winter.'

They watched hopefully for passing fishermen or tourist ferries, but nothing but sea birds crossed the horizon. As the sun rose, the sand bank shrunk steadily. Before long, it could barely have accommodated the two of them if they'd sat down and stretched their legs out.

'Ben,' Martine asked, 'do you think that when you're really frightened of things, you sort of attract them? I mean, you know how girls who are afraid of bats are always ending up with bats getting caught in their hair, while people who couldn't care less about them go their whole lives without seeing a single one? Well, I have a phobia about deep water and I seem to keep getting into situations where I have to face it.'

'I suppose it's possible,' Ben said. 'But maybe it's just your destiny.'

'To drown? Great.'

'No, silly. To be put into situations that would lead to you helping the dolphins, and to them helping you.'

Martine thought about it. About Mini, her life needlessly sacrificed; about the suffering in the eyes of the twenty-one dolphins beached at Dolphin Bay; of the whales in the Bahamas with bleeding eardrums. She thought, too, of the joy she'd experienced when the dolphin in Cape Town had swum away; of lying in the turquoise water gazing into the wise-innocent eyes of Little Storm; and of the night of the cyclone when she'd looked up to see a hundred dolphins coming through the wild waves, outlined in silver.

She and the others had helped the dolphins, but not nearly as much as the dolphins had helped her. Yes, they had saved her from the storm, but they'd also given her something far, far greater than that. They'd healed her. For the past two weeks, she had been so preoccupied with surviving that she wasn't even sure when it had happened. She didn't hurt any more. The knot of sadness that had dwelled inside her heart ever since the death of her mum and dad, six and half months earlier, was gone. She still felt very close to them – she felt as if they were watching over her as she stood on Death Island – but it was a good feeling, not a painful feeling.

Some of the fear left her and was replaced by the same sense of acceptance and optimism that had come over her when she first took in the severity of their predicament on the island. 'Ben,' she said, 'you know what's really weird? All of a sudden I'm not afraid any more. The dolphins will save us if they can find us, I know they will.'

'Then why don't we try telling them where we are?'

He took a deep breath and yelled as loudly as he could, 'Sun Dancer, Cookie, Ash, Thunder, Steel, Rain Dancer, Patch, Honey, Little Storm.' Martine did the same and then they took it in turns.

When they were almost hoarse from shouting, Martine took Ben's brown hand in her small white one and squeezed it hard. They were up to their ankles in water. He squeezed back and then they stood together, hand in trembling hand, looking out at the encroaching sea.

'If you could do it all again – I mean, everything that's happened in the last couple of weeks – would you do anything differently?' Ben asked.

'Yes,' said Martine. 'I'd tell my grandmother that I love her.'

30

Three days later, as she stared unseeingly from the window of the South African Airways plane carrying her and Ben back to Cape Town, those words came back to Martine. She had meant them with all her heart, but that didn't make the thought of returning to Sawubona any easier. She was almost more afraid of going home than she had been watching the approach of the wintry, shark-filled sea on Death Island. Who knew what conclusions her grandmother had come to in her absence? Maybe she'd decided that it was really rather pleasant not having a giraffe-mad eleven-year-old around. Maybe she liked having the house to herself again.

If so, there was not a lot Martine could do about it. She just had to hope that it wasn't too late to say sorry, and that whatever happened she wouldn't be sent away to England or some other place where she'd never again feel the African sun on her skin, ride her beloved giraffe, cuddle a lion cub, or smile at dolphins.

Ben nudged her. 'It doesn't seem real, does it? What happened to us, I mean. We swam with wild dolphins. We actually played with them. They carried us on their backs in a storm. They rescued us, then we rescued them, and then they rescued us right back again.' He laughed. 'It seems like a dream.'

'No,' said Martine, thinking of the shark nightmares that had started everything, 'it's much better than a dream.'

The first person Martine had seen after regaining consciousness in Maputo General Hospital was Alberto. The chef was sitting in a visitor's chair.

'Ah, Miss Martine, you are awake,' he said with a smile, the little ruby sparkling in his front tooth. 'You know, if you had mentioned you might be dropping into the Bazaruto Islands, I would have arranged for you to have a warmer welcome. Although from what I hear, you are quite the expert at building shelters!'

Alberto was wearing a white shirt, and the combination of that, his snowy hair, and the window behind him, framing a sky of pure and perfect blue, was such that Martine, who was still bleary after thirty-six hours of sleep, thought for a second that they were meeting in the afterlife. Then he added: 'You must have used your giraffe magic to talk to the dolphins and sharks, little miss. If it were not for them, you probably wouldn't be alive.' And it all came rushing back to her.

'Are the dolphins okay?' she asked in sudden panic. 'Did they beach themselves?'

'They are very well, thanks to you and your friend,' he assured her. 'I think they would want to know the same about the two of you.'

Martine sat up weakly. She was at the far end of a long hospital ward which smelled of disinfectant and roses. Nurses were gliding about, dispensing pills and trays of food. Ben was asleep in the bed beside her. A dazzling sun was casting stripy patterns on the green-tiled floor. A chubby-cheeked nurse came over, propped her up with pillows and took her temperature.

'Can ay bring you some tea and tosst?'

'Tosst?' queried Martine.

'Toast,' interpreted Alberto, and instructed the nurse, 'Miss Martine and the boy will have some coffee but no food, thank you.'

Martine opened her mouth to protest, but the chef winked at her and nodded in the direction of a large brown bag. No sooner had the nurse departed than he opened it up and produced four bacon and banana rolls, foiled-wrapped to keep them hot, and four pieces of coconut cake. The aroma of these delicacies roused Ben from his sleep, and he was soon sitting up munching on a roll. After he and Martine had been further revived with coffee and cake, Alberto filled them in on the events of the past couple of days.

As far as anyone could tell, they'd both lost consciousness within minutes of being swamped by the sea on Death Island. The doctor who'd examined them said that exhaustion, lack of food and cold water had combined to near-lethal effect.

'I was in the helicopter with the coastguard and Mr Rapier, searching for you,' explained Alberto. 'We had had no success until we saw this beautiful pattern from the air – more than a hundred dolphins in silver circles and, around them, a circle of black, white and speckled-yellow giants – whale sharks. We flew lower to take a closer look and there, in the middle of all these animals, were you and Ben.'

The cave painting, Martine thought. Every prediction on the Memory Room walls had come true.

'Mr Rapier was sure the whale sharks would swallow you whole, like canapés,' Alberto went on, 'but I told him that they are as gentle as porpoises and eat only plankton. But it is the dolphins who really saved you. You were lying across their backs, out of the cold water, and they were cradling you like babies. It was with great difficulty that we persuaded them that we were not there to hurt you.'

Ben and Martine listened in wonder, hardly able to wait to hear what came next.

'Why were you with Mr Rapier?' Martine wanted to

know. 'How did you guess where to look for us? We heard on the news that the rescue teams had been searching in the wrong place.'

'That is correct,' said Alberto. 'The morning after the cyclone, when none of you had been found, I contacted the coastguard's office and told them about my grandfather being helped by the dolphins. I said that maybe that had happened to you and your friends and the dolphins had swum against the current to take you to safety, but they just laughed at me. It was ten days before somebody told Mr Rapier about that possibility, and he contacted me right away to ask if I would help him search the Bazaruto Islands. We were on our way there when we heard from Ben's father that he'd received a message from you.'

'Dad got my message?' cried Ben. 'But he never responded.'

'He did, but he said you couldn't seem to hear him. You may have had the volume turned down on the radio.'

Ben looked sheepish. 'You might be right.'

'It didn't matter because he could hear you speaking so he could tell us that you were on Paradise Island and in great danger. We arrived too late to find you there, but luckily for us the young guard, Fernando, guessed that you might have been taken to Death Island. We did find your friend, Claudius, and he and his father were very overjoyed to see each other. It was quite sweet.'

'Don't let Claudius hear you say that,' Martine advised him.

'Did you manage to rescue our other friends?' asked Ben. 'Did Claudius tell you where to find them?'

'Yes, we took Claudius and flew straight away to Dugong Island, where we found them. There were quite a few tears, I can tell you. We brought them here to Maputo Hospital to be checked out. They were all fine, just very hungry and dehydrated. The two of you had already been carried here by air ambulance and you were sleeping, but they insisted on seeing you. They left something for you.'

Martine saw it then on the bedside locker – her survival kit. A piece of orange notepaper was taped to it. On it was scrawled, 'Cheers, guys. We owe you one. Martine, there'll be a new survival kit waiting for you in Cape Town, but we thought you might like this one as a souvenir. See you at Caracal Junior!!' They had all scribbled their signatures, and Sherilyn's had lots of x's after it.

There was a moment of silence while both Ben and Martine struggled to master their emotions.

Martine cleared her throat. 'Where are they now?'

'They went by plane to Cape Town this morning,' Alberto told her. 'Mr Rapier was going to take them for a fast food feast. Everyone except the big boy – Jake is it? He seemed very keen to get to a rugby match.'

'We still don't know what any of this was about,' Ben said. 'Why did nobody ever visit the island? What were the cables? Who was testing sonar?'

'Well,' said the chef, 'it is a simple story of greed. Ten years ago Dugong Island was bought by a very rich man from overseas. He had seen it once and loved it so much he wanted to preserve it. He rarely came to see it, but he allowed us islanders to picnic, fish or take our children there, so long as we left it the way we found it. Which we always did. We felt it was our heritage, too.

'Last year, this rich man died. His son came into possession of the island and he decided to put a hotel on it. He hired a man from the mainland, Marcos, from Maputo, to manage the project. Unlike his father, he thought of Dugong as private property and he wanted to put a stop to the islanders going there. Marcos's idea was to put underwater mines around the island. The police found out about it and there was a lot of trouble over it, but the son was going to invest millions of dollars and employ many workers, so they let the matter drop with a warning. Marcos recruited some contract workers and they set up a base in the old hotel on Paradise Island. All were from the mainland except for the young boy, Fernando, who had recently arrived in Maputo in search of work.'

Alberto paused to let the nurse take Ben's temperature, and clear away the coffee cups, crumbs and discarded foil. She gave the chef a disapproving glance.

'Perhaps all would have been well,' he continued after she'd gone, 'but planning permission for the lodge was very slow in coming and, two days after the contract workers began laying cables at Dugong Island, Marcos was contacted by the navy of a country whose name I will not mention. Because Dugong is the island furthest out into the Indian Ocean, they asked if he would allow them to test sonar in the waters surrounding it. He saw a chance for some extra cash. He didn't know that dolphins and whales might suffer because of the sonar and the stress caused by naval exercises. It was only when the son started to make enquiries about the lack of progress on Dugong Island that Marcos knew his golden goose would have to go. Still he gave permission for one last test – the one you told Ben's father about in your message.'

'Did anyone manage to stop it?' Ben said worriedly.

Alberto shook his head. 'Unfortunately not. It took time to find Marcos and to get him to admit what he was doing and who was carrying out the tests. The test went ahead before that happened. But we did organize for around thirty islanders to go to Dugong and wait there in case the dolphins tried to get onto the beach. But none came. It seems that every dolphin in the area was at Death Island when the test happened.'

Martine stared at him. 'So by saving us they actually saved themselves?' she said.

Alberto shrugged. 'We will never know. But it looks that way.'

'Do you think it will make a difference?' Martine said. 'Will navies around the world stop using LFA sonar if they know that it's contributing to dolphin deaths?'

'I'm not sure about that,' responded Alberto. 'On the news this morning, they were saying they needed to wait for more scientific evidence, more proof, before they acted. But our own government is talking of banning it in these waters, so at least you will know you have helped to create one sanctuary for dolphins and whales.'

'What happens now to the reward money?' Ben said. 'I take it that the skipper and his friends will not be getting it.'

'Mr Rapier met with the island chiefs yesterday and he has decided that half the money should go to build a new school on Benguerra Island. The other half, he and I are going to use to set up a restaurant on Benguerra. I've already offered Fernando a job as my sous-chef. We need bright young men like him on the islands.'

Alberto stood up to leave then. He was halfway down the ward when he remembered something and came back. 'I'm very sorry, Miss Martine, I should have told you this first, not last. We've had a message from your grandmother to say that she is so looking forward to seeing you.'

Now, as the plane thudded onto the runway and the engines screamed, the nauseous feeling in Martine's stomach intensified. Was her grandmother really looking forward to seeing her or was she dreading it? Was she scared too?

Inside the terminal, she and Ben, wearing colourful sweatshirts and cotton trousers donated by a Bazaruto Archipelago lodge (their own clothes had apparently disintegrated in the hospital washing machine), were escorted through the baggage hall by the flight attendant who had taken care of them since Maputo. Since they had no luggage to collect (their bags had returned to Cape Town on the *Sea Kestrel*), they thanked her and prepared to go into the arrivals hall.

Martine turned to Ben. How did you say goodbye to someone with whom you'd nearly died twice?

He was thinking the same thing, so they shuffled their feet and looked at the ground awkwardly before deciding on a quick hug.

'Everything's going to work out fine, you know,' Ben said. Martine had told him about the row with her grandmother when they were waiting for morning on Paradise Island.

'I s'pose,' mumbled Martine. 'I mean, I hope so.'

He reached out and touched her arm. 'It sounds mad, but I had a great time. Thanks for being my friend. There's no one in the world I'd rather be marooned on a desert island with!'

Martine couldn't help smiling. 'Same here. You're the best friend I've ever had – well, apart from Jemmy.'

Ben grinned. 'That's all right. I don't mind being second to a giraffe.'

31

Tendai was waiting in the arrivals hall, his khaki game ranger clothes and general stillness – the stillness of a man who spent a lot of time in nature – setting him apart from the stressed tourist hordes at the airport. He swept Martine up in his arms and whirled her around, his booming laugh causing people to stop and stare.

'You gave us a few sleepless nights, little one,' he said.

'Us?' queried Martine. She didn't know if she was relieved or devastated that Gwyn Thomas wasn't there to greet her.

Tendai put her down. 'Don't be too disappointed that

your grandmother hasn't come to the airport,' he said. 'This has been hard on her.'

What about me? Martine thought. I'm the one who nearly drowned, came close to being eaten by sharks, narrowly avoided being blown up by an undersea mine, and was left to die on Death Island. Whatever had been going on at Sawubona could hardly have been worse than that.

On the drive back home, Tendai talked to her about the game reserve, updating her on the progress of the sanctuary animals and describing a recent addition: a caracal kitten with a sore paw. 'The giraffe has been pining for you, little one,' he said. 'He hasn't left the waterhole in days. The visitors have been asking why the white giant is so sad.'

Martine couldn't bear the idea of Jemmy being unhappy but it was a nice feeling to know that he'd missed her. Then she remembered that she was banned from riding him.

To keep her mind off what was to come, she told Tendai about some of her adventures on the island. When she thanked him for his advice about keeping the survival kit with her at all times, and told him that that and the pouch he'd given her had helped to save seven lives, he looked proud enough to burst.

An hour and a half later they passed under Sawubona's black arch, and Tendai guided the jeep down the long sandy road to the main house. A white van was parked in the driveway. Martine climbed nervously out of the jeep. She could hear her grandmother's voice in the hallway. 'Quickly,' she was saying to someone. 'We haven't got much time.'

The door was shoved open and two men in overalls appeared. They were carrying Martine's bed. They nodded to Tendai and Martine, loaded the bed onto the back of the van and drove away.

Martine's knees nearly gave way. Was she going to be sent back to England after all?

Gwyn Thomas came out onto the front step. She was pale and seemed to have lost weight. 'Martine!' she cried, rushing over to embrace her. 'I didn't hear you arrive. Look at you! I was expecting a scruffy castaway, but you look so brown and healthy. Grace will definitely want to feed you up though! Come inside. I know you must be exhausted, but I have a surprise for you.'

Martine wriggled out of her grandmother's arms and stood stiffly, but she refused to cry. If she had to go, she would go proudly with her head held high, and she would not leave without saying goodbye to Jemmy. 'I already know what the surprise is,' she said.

Her grandmother looked sharply at Tendai. 'Did you say something?' she accused.

'I said nothing, Mrs Thomas,' the game warden protested. 'Nothing at all.'

When the roar of Tendai's jeep faded, Gwyn Thomas turned and went inside. Martine followed her with dread in her heart. The thought of leaving this lovely, serene house, with its welcoming fireplace and wooden beams and oil paintings of cheetahs and elephants, was agony. Warrior and Shelby, the cats, were snuggled in a worn leather armchair. Her grandmother was halfway up the stairs to Martine's room, her shoes clumping on the wooden stairs.

Martine climbed slowly after her. She walked into her room and stopped short. It had been transformed! The walls had been freshly whitewashed, and there was a new bed by the window, spread with a blue duvet decorated with African batik images of a white giraffe. Above the bookcase were three large silver-framed photographs: one of Martine and her parents laughing on a beach in Cornwall, one of Jemmy by the waterhole, and one of a pod of dolphins playing in the waves.

'I was going to redecorate your room as your Christmas present,' her grandmother said, 'but when you went missing I nearly went out of my mind. I couldn't sleep I was in such a state. Grace persuaded me to do this to pass the time. One of Grace's nieces is a fine arts student at the University of Cape Town and she hand-made the batik giraffe for the duvet cover.'

Despite her resolution, Martine's eyes filled with tears. 'Thank you. It's wonderful. I'm so sorry. I thought that you were sending me away.'

'I know what you thought,' her grandmother said. 'And I don't blame you. I can be a stubborn old woman at times. I cursed myself for letting you go away without resolving our row, and of course once you were on the ship I couldn't contact you. My husband had a very wise saying, "Never go to sleep on an argument." Unfortunately, in the heat of the moment, I forgot that. I was just so afraid that you'd steal out at night once too often and that something would happen to you and I'd lose you like I lost your mum. But I'm sorry for hurting you. Please forgive me.'

She opened her arms and Martine flew into them and they held each other like they'd never let go.

'I'm sorry too,' Martine told her. 'I'm sorry for disobeying you and I'm really, really sorry for saying what I said. I didn't mean it.'

They stepped apart. 'Have I told you how much I love you?' Gwyn Thomas said.

'No.' Martine responded shyly.

'Well, I do. You mean more to me than anything else in the world.'

'Really?'

'Yes, really.'

'Well, I . . . '

'It's okay,' said her grandmother, suddenly embarrassed. 'I know without you having to say it.'

'But I want to,' Martine told her. 'I learned on the island that it's important to say things when you have the chance. I love you, too, and I'm very, very happy to be home with you.'

Her grandmother's reserve got the better of her then, and she ruffled Martine's hair and muttered something about getting dinner started. Martine pretended that she was organizing herself to take a shower. She was desperate to see the white giraffe, but she didn't want to burst the bubble.

Her grandmother lingered at the door. 'Hadn't you better get your boots and jeans on if you're going to go for a ride?' she asked, smiling.

'But you told me I was banned from riding him?'

'You'd better hurry up in case I change my mind. I meant what I said – absolutely no sneaking out at night. But I can't stop you riding the white giraffe. The two of you are inseparable. Jemmy is your soul-mate. You need each other.'

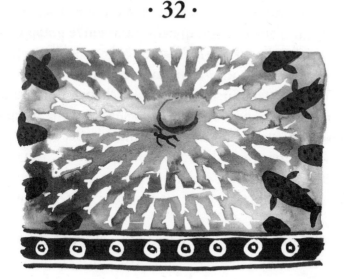

For Martine, who had on numerous occasions over the past two weeks thought she'd never see the white giraffe again, the moment when she caught sight of him waiting for her at the waterhole was something that she'd always treasure.

It was hard to tell who was more excited. Jemmy cantered over to her as exuberantly as a pony, lowered his silver head, nuzzled her and made his musical fluttering sound, while Martine spent ages just stroking his silky coat, telling him off for not eating properly, and trying to explain about the storm and the dolphins and how she'd thought about him every minute on the island. Then she climbed onto his sloping, silky back and became a part of him again.

As soon as she was out of sight of the house, she urged him into a flat-out gallop across the golden savannah. Ordinarily, she was careful not to go too fast in daylight in case her grandmother caught sight of her and decided giraffe-riding was a recipe for broken bones, but this afternoon she was on a mission. Not even a snarling lioness, woken from her slumber in the winter sunshine, could detain her.

When she reached the trees near the barren clearing, she halted Jemmy, and spent several minutes scanning the area for prying eyes. Visiting the Secret Valley was another thing she'd resolved never to do in the daytime, but that, too, couldn't be helped. Once through the thorny wall that guarded the crevice, she slid down the white giraffe's neck as if she was shooting down a waterslide, turned on her torch, and positively ran down the tunnel, only slowing to tiptoe through the bats' home in the antechamber.

Grace was in the Memory Room, as Martine had known she would be. She was sitting on the flat rock that served as a sort of bench, wearing Zulu traditional dress and drinking from a flask of *rooibos* tea. When Martine ran in, she gave a cry of delight and enveloped her in a massive hug. 'You're arl bones,' Grace said when they finally parted. 'What ya been eatin' on that island? Bet ya wished you had summa Grace's good food.'

Martine giggled. 'Oh, Grace,' she said, still a little breathless after having the air almost crushed from her lungs, 'I missed more than just your food. When I ended up alone on the island because of some stupid things I said and did, and I felt like everyone in the world was disappointed in me, I wished that you were there to give me a hug and tell me something wise to make everything all right.'

Grace's eyes shone but she didn't say anything. She patted the rock beside her and poured Martine a cup of *rooibos*. They sat there sipping the hot red tea in the light of two torches, surrounded by glowing copper scenes of centuries-old Bushmen life.

After a while Martine said, 'You knew I would be back, didn't you?'

Grace smiled, revealing bright pink gums. 'Sure did, chile. I done tole your grandmamma everythin' would be all right, but she don't ever believe me when I say the bones don't lie. I tole her that the dolphins would see no harm would come to ya.'

'But how did you *know*?' Martine probed. 'How could you know about the dolphins? I mean, if I'd understood what you meant about the boat fence, we would never have ended up in the sea.'

But the *sangoma* just laughed and changed the subject. 'That boy, Claudius, he came to see me yesterday.'

Martine stared at her in disbelief. 'Claudius?! Why? What did he want?'

She couldn't for the life of her imagine how Claudius, of all people, had managed to track Grace down. But it seems he had. Not only that, but he'd impressed her by giving her a magnificent bouquet of flowers to thank her for providing Martine with the plant which saved his life.

'I tole him, that ugly thing! Who knew it would come to any good? It's been followin' me around like a bad smell for years. Every time I dig it out of my garden, it grow back again. Many times I wanted to t'row it in the trash but I's afeared that granny was goin' to come back and haunt me. Then I thought, I'll jest give it to Martine to take on har journey. Maybe she can lose it in the sea.'

'Are you serious?' Martine wasn't sure if this was Grace's idea of a joke. 'Is it something your Caribbean grandmother gave you? You really didn't know that one of the kids on the trip would get stung and need its sap to survive?'

'Chile,' Grace said warmly, 'this is *your* destiny. You have your gift. I weren't the one on the island.'

Martine smothered a sigh. She knew her questions would never really be answered. And as frustrating as that was, she would have to let it go.

'What did you think of Claudius?' she asked, unable to suppress a grin at the thought of Claudius, doubtless scrubbed-up and in his best clothes, sitting among the chickens that pecked around Grace's living room.

'He's a good boy,' Grace told her. 'He done chosen the wrong path before but he learn from that and now maybe if he remember that money can't always buy what matters in this life, he'll grow into a fine young man.'

Martine stood up and went over to examine the two ocean paintings. It felt peculiar to look at them after their predictions had come true. And they were remarkably accurate. Even the sharks were not just painted as random sharks but had the yellow and white markings which identified them as whale sharks.

'You know, Grace,' she said, 'the San people, or the forefathers, or whoever it was who created these pictures, they saw nearly everything that was to come. They even knew the number of beached dolphins, twenty-one, and the species of shark and that there were at least a hundred dolphins in rings surrounding us. They just got one thing wrong. There were two of us on Death Island – my friend Ben and me. There should be two swimmers in this picture and there's only one.'

'Are ya, sure, chile?' Grace said. 'Look closely.'

Martine did and she still saw only one swimmer. Then she noticed that there was a flake of shimmering rock, almost like mica, clinging to the centre of the painting. She peeled it away. Beneath it was the second swimmer.

Martine's blood ran cold. As much as she loved the cave, the knowledge that someone, centuries ago, could have predicted her future in such detail, gave her chills. Before Martine had got to know Ben, when she was still isolated at school, Grace had told her that she would find the friend she sought in the last place she looked. And so it had proven. So maybe Ben himself was part of everything. Maybe everything was linked, even their friendship.

'That's spooky,' Martine said. 'Do you think that the second swimmer was there all the time or do you think . . . I know it sounds weird, but do you think it could have just appeared recently, by some kind of Bushmen magic?'

Grace gave her a strange smile. 'I tole you before, chile, everythin' is already written, but only time and experience will give you the eyes to see it.'

To celebrate their safe return, Gwyn Thomas suggested to Ben's mum and dad that the five of them have lunch the following Sunday at the beach kitchen in Uiserfontein, the place where Martine had healed the dolphin. It was usually shut all winter, but there had been a run of unseasonably mild weather and Gwyn Thomas had seen an advert announcing it would be open for the next two weekends.

Martine had been introduced to Ben's parents at the airport, and she'd found his Zulu father almost as quiet as his son was, although he exuded an unmistakable authority. In appearance, though, they were nothing alike. Where Ben was small and wiry, Dumisani was well over six feet, with a dignified bearing, his muscles so broad and defined they might have been sculpted. Ben's Indian mother, Sinita, by contrast, was tiny, talkative, and delicately beautiful, with long glossy black hair which smelled of coconut. It was she who Ben resembled most closely. But his inner strength, thought Martine, his inner strength came from Dumisani.

The Khumalos picked Martine and Gwyn Thomas up from Sawubona in an old station wagon, stopping briefly to meet Tendai, Jemmy and Grace. Jemmy still refused to allow anyone but Martine to touch him, but he hovered near enough for them to appreciate his lustrous white coat and great height.

'He *looks* like a creature of legend,' Dumisani remarked. 'A wonder horse.'

For once Grace said little, although she was very interested to meet Ben. When she came to the car to say goodbye, she hugged him as if she'd always known him and Martine was pleased to see that he didn't act embarrassed, like most boys his age would have done. Instead he looked Grace in the eye and there was a respectful familiarity in the way he spoke, as if he, too, felt a kinship with her.

Two hours later, they pulled into the carpark at Uiserfontein. It was a fine, fresh afternoon. Heathery plants in rich purples and maroons, their colours startling against the creamy sand, crowded up to the dunes, and sea birds wheeled above the waves. They walked along a path of crushed shells to the restaurant and Martine found, to her delight, that it really was a beach kitchen. Rustic tables were set on a wooden deck on the sand's edge, just beyond the reach of the waves, and even the ovens were open to the elements. The aroma of baking bread greeted them. The sunshine took the edge off the winter chill, and the sky was so blue it seemed infinite.

Soon they were tucking into one of the best meals Martine had ever eaten. There was a delicious seafood bisque to start, accompanied by hot, doughy bread baked in clay ovens. After an interval, big bowls of Greek salad, coleslaw and watermelon appeared, followed by the main attraction – snoek, a smoked game fish. Martine had so many plates of it she was sure that she'd have to be transported back to the car in a wheelbarrow!

While they ate, Sinita reminisced about her early life as a dancer in Rajasthan and told them about Pushkar, a festival held once a year, where people came from all over India to trade silks, crafts and jewellery, and to race camels and magnificent Arab horses from the Punjab. It was a world away from the experiences Martine had had so far and it made her realize how much more of the planet there was to see. 'You will travel to the ends of the earth and have a whole lotta adventures before you're done,' Grace had once told her. Martine liked the sound of that, but she wasn't so sure about the 'many, many challenges' which Grace had mentioned would also be coming her way. She'd had enough challenges in the past six months to last a lifetime.

After the main course, Gwyn Thomas suggested that

they go for a walk in an effort to make room for dessert – *koeksisters,* twists of deep-fried batter, drenched in syrup. Martine was too full and too sleepily contented to talk, so she dawdled along the fringes of the surf while the others went ahead. When she reached the spot where she'd healed the dolphin, she stopped and stared out to sea. She was thrilled to be home at Sawubona with Jemmy, but that didn't mean that she missed the dolphins any less. Everything about them was graceful and smart and a celebration of each precious moment of life. Dolphins made it easy to feel happy.

'Funny thing about dolphins,' the kite surfer had said, 'ever noticed that you can't help smiling when you're around them?' And she had.

At that exact moment a dolphin jumped in the bay. Martine wondered if it was the dolphin she'd helped. It was incredibly unlikely, but then so many fantastical things had happened to her recently nothing would have surprised her. But although she fixed her eyes on the patch of ocean where she fancied she'd seen him, he didn't reappear, and after a while Martine came to the conclusion that it was probably wishful thinking on her part.

She was about to walk on when she noticed something drawn on the sand. It was a leopard. Every detail of it was lovingly recreated, right down to its claws and whiskers, and it was full-size, drawn to scale. At least, she thought it was. It seemed an extra large leopard. Its teeth were bared in a snarl and there was something coiled about it, as if it was poised to attack.

It was so realistic that Martine took a step back. She

checked behind her, wondering where the artist was. She hadn't seen anyone on the shoreline. The tide was coming in and the image was too crisp and sharp to have been there more than a few minutes. But, apart from Ben, his parents and Gwyn Thomas, and a couple of fishermen unloading their catch in the distance, the beach was empty.

'Grandmother! Ben! Come and have a look at this,' she called.

Ben sprinted over, and his parents and Gwyn Thomas followed more slowly. 'What is it?' he asked when he reached her. 'What have you seen?'

Martine went to show him and halted in disbelief. In the few seconds that her back had been turned, a wave had rushed in and washed the pale sand smooth. Flecks of glistening foam marked its path. Not a trace of the leopard remained.

A shiver went through Martine and, at the back of her mind, a warning bell tolled.

'What is it?' Ben asked again.

'It's nothing,' Martine said. 'I made a mistake. It must have been a trick of the light.'

'Come,' urged her grandmother, walking up to her and putting an arm around her shoulders, 'it's getting cold now. Look at you! You're covered in goosebumps. Let's go in for some coffee and *koeksisters*.'

Out in the bay, a dolphin breached the waves, gave a flick of its tail and dived deep again.

AUTHOR'S NOTE

A few years ago, I went to Monkey Mia in Shark's Bay, Western Australia, where I'd heard it was possible to swim with wild dolphins. On arrival, I found that it wasn't quite so simple. There was no actual swimming involved. We just stood knee-deep in the sea stroking the dolphins, or took turns, with other tourists, to feed them.

Of course, that was amazing enough. The thing that really struck me was the dolphins' eyes. They'd lie on their sides gazing up, and when I stared back it was like looking into eyes as innocent as those of a new-born baby and, simultaneously, those of the wisest creature on earth. Their gaze was all-knowing. It seemed to me that the dolphins understood more than we ever could. Their skin was remarkable too! I had expected it to be cold and slightly slimy. Instead, it was silky-smooth and beautiful to touch and I could feel their powerful muscles rippling underneath.

This made me want to swim with them more desperately than ever. I pleaded with the owners of the resort and even the research scientists to make my dream come true, but they insisted it wasn't possible. One evening I was sitting alone on the beach watching the sunset turn the water to molten gold when a fishing boat came in, followed by a mother dolphin, known at Monkey Mia as Nicky, and her calf. Well, I didn't hesitate. I dived into the sea in my shorts and T-shirt and swum out a little distance from them. Nicky had a reputation for being greedy and was preoccupied with waiting for stray fish from the fishing boat, but I noticed her calf watching me inquisitively.

After a couple of minutes, he started to swim in my direction. The water is very buoyant in that part of Australia, so I lay on my stomach and stretched my arms out and, slowly and very shyly, he moved closer. Eventually we were only a couple of inches apart. That moment, lying in the red-gold sea, gazing into the wise-innocent eyes of a baby dolphin, was unforgettable. I borrowed from it for the scene in *Dolphin Song* where Martine first swims with Little Storm.

My fascination with dolphins didn't end with my visit to Monkey Mia. I was always trying to find an opportunity to get close to them again, and whenever I read about dolphin and whale strandings, most of which seem to end in tragedy, it broke my heart. As the number of animals involved in these strandings increased, I started to wonder what caused it, what the common denominator might be.

Then I heard that the testing of low-frequency active sonar had been directly linked to the deaths of whales in the Bahamas. Since that day, the weight of evidence gathered by marine scientists and conservationists proving – beyond doubt in many cases – that active sonar is linked to the strandings of whales (particularly species such as beaked whales), has continued to mount.

Forced to surface too quickly, the whales die of a condition similar to the bends in humans and are frequently found with bleeding brains and ears. Dolphin experts are divided over whether the increased use of sonar is directly responsible for the rise in beachings of dolphins, or whether activity such as naval exercises in the area causes them so much stress and fear that they literally try to flee the ocean. Either way the outcome is the same.

Reading about the impact of sonar testing on marine mammals gave me the idea for *Dolphin Song*. I knew I wanted it to be about a school trip that goes disastrously wrong, and when my mum, who lives in South Africa's Western Cape, close to Martine's fictional home, Sawubona, started sending me regular reports on the miracle of nature that is the Sardine Run, that provided a perfect reason for a school adventure. All I needed was a location. I wanted to find a remote African island which was still home to wild dolphins. I'd heard that Mozambique's Bazaruto Archipelago was such a place, and I decided to go to see it for myself.

There are five main islands in the Bazaruto Archipelago, so I hope the Mozambicans won't mind that I've taken the liberty of adding a sixth, Dugong, for the purposes of my story. However, the Death Island sandbar and other islands mentioned – Benguerra, Bazaruto, and Santa Carolina, with its eerie, abandoned hotel, which I explored – all exist. They are a true African paradise. The sand is so clean that it squeaks when you walk, the water is aquamarine, and the islanders are extremely proud that their islands are friendly and free of crime.

The islands also happen to be home to several hundred-strong pods of dolphins. Late one afternoon a boatman took me out in a rubber dinghy to look for them. We found them close to the reef hunting shoals of little fish. The sight of their lithe, graceful bodies glinting in the clear water as they darted like quicksilver all around us, surfacing periodically to take a puff of oxygen, was beyond beautiful. This time I felt no urge to swim with them. I was content to watch dolphins at play in their natural environment; dolphins left alone to be free. I prayed that sonar testing would never find its way to the Bazaruto Islands as it does in *Dolphin Song*.

Writing this book and being able to spend months immersed in a world of dolphins was one of the best experiences of my life. In *Dolphin Song*, Martine's gift allows her and her friends to help twenty-one beached dolphins and return all but one to the sea. In real life, dolphins and whales rely on marine welfare organizations and ordinary people like you and me to take an interest in them and try to protect them.

We only have one planet. Let's do our best to care for it.

Lauren St John
London 2007

The Last Leopard, the sequel to *Dolphin Song*
is now available.
Here is a preview of the first chapter.

· 1 ·

Dawn was casting spun-gold threads across a rosy sky over Sawubona Game Reserve as Martine Allen took a last look around to ensure there weren't any witnesses, leaned forward like a jockey on the track, wound her fingers through a tangle of silver mane, and cried, 'Go, Jemmy, go!'

The white giraffe sprang forward so suddenly that she was almost unseated, but she recovered and, wrapping her arms around his neck, quickly adjusted to the familiar rhythm of Jemmy's rocking-horse stride. They swept past the dam and a herd of bubble-blowing hippos, past a flock of startled egrets lifting from the trees like white glitter, and out onto the open savannah plain. An early morning African chorus of doves, crickets and go-away birds provided a soundtrack.

For a long time Martine had only ever ridden Jemmy at night and in secret, but when her grandmother had found out about their nocturnal adventures she'd promptly banned them, on the grounds that the game reserve's deadliest animals were all in search of dinner after dark and there was nothing they'd like more than to feast on a giraffe-riding eleven-year-old. For a while Martine had defied her, but after several close calls and one terrible row with her grandmother, she had come to accept that Gwyn Thomas was right. When lions were on the hunt, the game reserve was best avoided.

Another of Gwyn Thomas's rules was that Martine ride sedately at all times. 'No faster than a trot and, in fact, I'd rather you stuck to a walk,' she'd counselled sternly.

Martine had paid almost no attention. The way she saw it, Jemmy was a wild animal and it was only fair that he should have the freedom to do what came naturally, and if that meant tearing across the savannah at a giraffe's top speed of thirty-five kmph, well, there wasn't a lot she could do about it. It wasn't as if she had reins to stop him. Besides, what was the point of riding a giraffe if the most he was permitted to do was plod along like some arthritic pony from the local stables?

Jemmy clearly agreed. They flew across the grassy plain with the spring breeze singing in Martine's ears. 'Faster, Jemmy!' she yelled. 'Run for your life.' And she laughed out loud at the heart-pounding thrill of it, of racing a wild giraffe.

A streak of grey cut across her vision, accompanied by a furious, nasal squeal: '*Mmwheeeh!*'

Jemmy swerved. In the instant before her body parted company with the white giraffe's, Martine caught a glimpse of a warthog charging from its burrow, yellow tusks thrust forward. Had her arms not been wrapped so tightly around the giraffe's neck, she would have crashed ten feet to the ground. As it was, she just sort of swung under his chest like a human necklace. There she dangled while Jemmy pranced skittishly and the warthog, intent on defending her young, let out enraged squeals from below. Five baby warthogs milled around in bewilderment, spindly tails pointing heavenwards.

The pain in Martine's arms was nearly unbearable, but she dared not let go. She adored warthogs – warts, rough skin, pig ears and all – but their Hollywood movie star eyelashes didn't fool her. In a blink of those lashes, their tusks could reduce her limbs to bloody ribbons.

'Jemmy,' she said through gritted teeth, 'walk on. Good boy.'

Confused, the white giraffe started to lower his neck as he backed away from the warthog.

'No, Jemmy!' shrieked Martine as the warthog nipped at the toe of one of her boots. 'Walk! Walk on!'

Jemmy snatched his head up to evade the warthog's sharp tusks, and Martine was able to use the momentum to hook her legs around his neck. From there, she was able to haul herself onto his back and urge him into a sprint. Soon the warthog family was a grey blur in the distance, although the mother's grunts of triumph took longer to fade.

Martine rode the rest of the way home at a gentle walk, a rueful smile on her lips. That would teach her to show off – even if it was only to an audience of hippos. At the game reserve gate, Jemmy dipped his head and Martine slid down his silvery neck as though she was shooting down a waterslide. That, too, wasn't the safest way of dismounting, but it was fun. She gave the white giraffe a parting hug, and strolled through the mango trees to the thatched house.

In the kitchen, brown sugar-dusted tomatoes were turning to caramel in the frying pan. Martine's nose wrinkled appreciatively. She was starving. Six days a week her grandmother served up boiled eggs and toast, with the occasional bowl of cornflakes as light relief, but on Sundays and special days like this she made up for it by cooking delicious brunches or roasts or allowing Martine to go for a campfire breakfast on the escarpment with Tendai, the Zulu game warden.

Martine took off her boots on the back *stoep* and stepped inside barefoot. "Morning, grandmother," she said.

'Hello, Martine,' Gwyn Thomas said, closing the oven and standing upright. She wore a red-striped apron over a denim shirt. 'Wash your hands and come take a seat. Did you have a nice ride? Did Jemmy behave himself today?'

'Jemmy was an angel,' Martine responded loyally,

thinking: When does he ever *not* behave himself? It wasn't his fault if the warthog had woken up on the wrong side of her burrow.

There was a polite knock at the door.

'Ah, Ben,' said Gwyn Thomas with a smile, 'good timing. Breakfast is almost ready. Come and join us.'

'Thank you, ma'am,' said a clear young voice.

Martine turned to see a half-Zulu, half-Indian boy entering the kitchen a little shyly. He wore an army-green vest, heavy brown boots and ragged jeans – the only pair he owned since turning his others into shorts during an island adventure a little over a month earlier. He had glossy black hair and skin the colour of burnt honey and, though very slim – some might even say thin – he was sinewy and strong.

He rinsed his hands at the sink and sat down at the table. 'Have a bit of trouble with a warthog this morning, Martine?' he teased. 'You and Jemmy left skid marks all over the bush. The ground was so torn up it looked like the starting grid of the East Africa Safari car rally.'

'What happened?' demanded Gwyn Thomas. 'Were you going too fast, Martine? You know very well that you're expressly forbidden to gallop Jemmy. I won't have you breaking your neck on my watch. Ben, did the tracks show that she was going very fast?'

Martine glanced quickly at Ben. She knew that he knew she'd be in big trouble if she was caught racing the white giraffe, but she was also aware that he never lied about anything. Nor would she expect him to. She braced herself for a scolding and a temporary ban on riding Jemmy. Just her luck. And on the first day of the school holidays, too.

'I think . . . ' Ben shifted uncomfortably in his chair.

Her grandmother put her hands on her hips. 'You think what? Out with it, Ben.'

' . . . I think the toast is burning,' Ben said brightly.

Gwyn Thomas jumped up and seized the smoking grill pan, blowing on it to put out the flames licking at the four bits of charcoal that had once been bread. Just then the oven timer started beeping to indicate that the mushrooms were done and Martine noticed the tomatoes were starting to smoke. By the time they'd managed to rescue their charred breakfast, make more toast and hastily scramble a few eggs to go with it, her grandmother appeared to have forgotten about Martine's dangerous riding.

Ben distracted her further by relaying a warthog story Tendai had told him that morning, about an apprentice hunter he'd met during his game ranger studies. One afternoon the young hunter decided to entertain the other apprentices and demonstrate his bravery by tormenting a warthog in a game enclosure just for the fun of seeing her riled. He planned to hop over the fence if she came after him.

'Only problem was, the fence was electric!' reported Ben with a grin. 'The hunter was hanging on for twenty minutes, sort of sizzling, before she got bored and went away.'

Martine, whose arms still ached from her own encounter with an exasperated warthog, laughed, but not quite as hard as her grandmother.

'What do the two of you have planned for the holidays?' asked Gwyn Thomas, pouring them each a glass of paw paw juice. 'Apart, Martine, from riding the white giraffe very, very slowly.' She gave her granddaughter a meaningful glance, indicating that she hadn't forgotten what Ben had said but was prepared to let it go just this once.

Martine smiled gratefully. 'Don't worry,' she said, 'I'll be riding so slowly that even tortoises will overtake us.'

When she wasn't doing that she was hoping to brush up on her bushcraft skills and paint watercolours of the animals in Sawubona's sanctuary, a hospital and holding area for injured wildlife and new arrivals to the game reserve.

Ben, meanwhile, had his parents' permission to spend almost the whole holidays at Sawubona, studying under Tendai as an apprentice tracker.

When Martine first met Ben, he'd been almost completely silent, never speaking a word to anyone but her and his parents. Most kids at school had believed he was dumb. Some still did. But at Sawubona he seemed to really enjoy chatting to Tendai, Gwyn Thomas or anyone else who happened to be around.

As she listened to him describe his morning in the reserve, Martine absent-mindedly speared the last few potatoes on her plate and took in the scene in the kitchen. Eight months ago, her mum and dad had been killed in a fire in England on New Year's Eve and she'd been shipped like a parcel off to Africa to live with a strict grandmother she hadn't even known existed. For the first month or two Martine had been convinced she would never be happy again. Yet here she was sitting contentedly at the breakfast table with that same grandmother who, after a rocky start, had become one of her very favourite people, and with Ben, her best friend in the world apart from Jemmy.

Through the open doorway Martine could see zebras splashing around the distant waterhole. She would never stop missing her parents, but it definitely helped that her new home was one of the most lovely game reserves in South Africa's Western Cape and that she could ride through it on her own white giraffe and get close enough to zebras and elephants to touch them. She preferred the weather in Africa too. It was early but already the sun was spilling orange across the kitchen tiles and Shelby, the ginger cat, was stretched out in its warmth.

The telephone trilled loudly, making them jump. Gwyn Thomas checked her watch and frowned. 'It's barely seven o'clock. I wonder who's calling us so early on a Saturday morning.'

She went into the living room to answer it. Evidently the line was a bad one because she had to speak very loudly.

'Sadie!' she cried, her voice carrying clearly. 'What a lovely surprise. How nice to hear from you. How are things at Black Eagle Lodge . . . ? Oh, no. Oh, surely not. I'm very sorry to hear that. Well, if there's anything I can do, don't hesitate to let me know. *Excuse me?* Oh. OHHH . . . !'

Ben and Martine looked at each other, and Ben raised an eyebrow. 'Sounds like trouble,' he murmured.

'Uh, uh, yes, I understand,' Gwyn Thomas was saying. 'No, no, it's not an imposition. Please don't think that for a minute. In fact, the timing couldn't be better. We're on our way. Try not to worry. We'll see you very soon. Take care of yourself in the meanwhile.'

There was the sound of the receiver being replaced, followed by a long silence. When she returned to the kitchen, Gwyn Thomas's face was sober. 'Martine, Ben,' she said, 'I'm afraid you're both going to have to put your plans on hold. Martine, we leave first thing in the morning. We'll be gone for a month. We're going to Zimbabwe.'